# WHEN MAN WAS YOUNG

## STEPHEN BROOKE

Arachis Press 2021

When Man Was Young ©2021 Stephen Brooke

ISBN 978-1-937745-76-9

Arachis Press
4803 Peanut Road
Graceville, FL 32440
http://arachispress.com

The title of this book comes from a poem by Stephen Brooke. It is included in his collection *Dreamwinds*.

## An Age Ago

There was a sea, a nameless, ice-bound sea,
and we were there; in some forgotten age,
I held you close upon its ancient shore.

I brought the prizes of primeval hunts;
across an empty glacial land I came
to lay before you soft luxurious pelts.

Do you remember star-filled nights we met,
among the shadowed forest hills, to pledge
eternal love beneath a sky still new?

A little while we shared in that cold time
when man was young; yet, there we lived and died
and loved, an age ago, when you were mine.

*Stephen Brooke ©1986*

# PART I.
# AN AGE AGO

## 1.

IT WASN'T AS COLD as I expected, despite being the Ice Age. Yes, we had been told it would be summer. The air was heavily perfumed by the blooms in the meadow around us, a lush lawn spreading across the hills and rising to the low pale cliffs. A few stunted-looking trees stood. Larch, I suspected. The brochure had mentioned them.

There were crows. The only other living creatures were tiny and buzzed in swarms around us. The animal skins we wore were not sufficient to keep the mosquitoes at bay. We had been assured the attire was appropriate to the Paleolithic.

"Our destination is a cave in a valley over that way," said our guide, pointing more or less to the east. "The next valley over. I have visited this cave more than once and I am always new to those who live there."

So off we set to meet Neanderthal women.

* * *

'Temporal Sex Tourism' is what the technicians had called it, certainly a bit tongue in cheek. Travel to the past to have sex. It had become the most popular use of time travel—and one which helped finance serious research into the past.

It had been demonstrated to everyone's satisfaction—almost everyone's—that visiting the past had no effect on the present. "You see," we were told during our orientation, "we have traveled to the same time and place over and over, and found no evidence we had ever been there. Apparently, the paradoxes involved are not permitted. The future can't change the past."

A hand went up. "Isn't there a theory that it creates a new timeline?" asked Bob. He was a younger man. The other three of us were middle-aged. All male.

Our lecturer nodded. She had probably heard this question a time or two before. "It is only a theory. There is no proof."

"Nor likely ever to be," added Mr. Palit, our guide on this trip. "It makes no practical difference. We will return to the world we left." He had been content to sit to one side, so far. Now he stepped forward. "Ms. Witkos has covered all the basics," he said. "Any other questions before we begin gearing up?"

"It—it really doesn't matter what we do there?" This from a balding man who had introduced himself as Felipe. The four of us were using our given names. It was supposed to promote cama-raderie.

"Only to your conscience," replied Palit. "Be aware, however, I will not permit any intentional cruelty."

It was an intriguing thought. Once we entered the past, none of our actions had any consequences. We'd all heard of those who had abused this complete liberty. Or could it truly be called abuse if none of it mattered?

In theory, I could even slaughter my fellow time travelers. However, they would pop back here as soon as it happened, none the worse, and report me! So I had been told anyway. Oddly, their bodies would remain in the past—there would be two of them, one alive, one dead. That had been a big surprise, apparently, the first time someone died while time traveling. The travelers had returned, bearing their bad news, only to be greeted by the man they thought had died.

Yeah, sort of like that famous cat in the box. But different. Apparently, the whole underpinning of time travel relied on some quantum sleight of hand of that sort. Don't expect me to know the science. I'm not sure even the scientists know it.

Punishment for any transgression? We had all posted sizable bonds that could be forfeited. That in addition to the hefty fee we had paid to come. It took money to be a time-traveling tourist.

"An observer has been added to our party," Palit went on. "She'll join us when we launch."

She? We gave each other furtive, sidelong looks. Having a woman along was definitely nothing any of us wanted, given our purpose in traveling sixty thousand years into the past.

"You all agreed to this in the contracts you signed," added Ms. Witkos.

Palit grinned at us. "She won't get in the way, I promise you. Research is her only interest. Curiosity, which I suspect is also the real reason you are here."

I couldn't argue with that. As for the others, I couldn't say.

\* \* \*

Katherine Chebab—Doctor Chebab—proved to be a diminutive, dark-haired woman, possibly in her thirties. We avoided looking at her in her Neanderthal attire, which consisted of a hide skirt and no top. It was likely we'd get use to it. All the women dressed that way where we were going. We were dressed that way ourselves.

Palit lectured as we hiked across the hills. Or Jad, as he told us to call him, short for Jadunath. "There's a variety of heather here," he said, "especially higher on the slopes." He waved an arm in their direction. They rose to low but steep rock cliffs and outcroppings here and there. "You won't find that in Italy in our time. Grasses and wildflowers predominate down here." We spied what were some sort of deer in the distance. They observed us a while before returning to their grazing.

We all knew the material. We were supposed to, anyway. I did not know how conscientious my fellow time travelers had been. But we had prepared. There had been a fitness test before they would take our money and we had trained some since. We had studied our destination, even learned a little of the bewilderingly complex language. Jad was said to speak it pretty well or as well as could be expected. I wondered if Chebab knew any of it.

And we had all grown beards to fit in. No clean-shaven Neanderthals allowed.

"As you know," Jad continued, "we are visiting a group of

women and children. Their men are presumed to be dead. We have observed them at a later time and know they never return."

"And this group disappears too," spoke Bob.

"They do. Perhaps they wandered off looking for a better place to live. Perhaps cold and privation killed them all. We don't know."

"If I was given permission to revisit them at the proper time we might find out," said Chebab.

"Not my decision, Doctor," Palit told her, "but I doubt the funds would be available. I *am* interested in how they'll respond to a woman in our party. That's a first."

"Me too. Call me Kat since the rest of you are using your first names."

Our guide only nodded to that. "I do know they will be, um, apprehensive when we show ourselves. For all they know we might intend to eat them."

"And they've never seen anyone who looks like us," said Felipe.

"Won't be able to tell the difference at a distance," Yukey told him. That was Euclid Ball, a large, powerful looking—albeit some of that largeness was around his middle—man. He headed a big construction firm, I understood. We all were pretty much successful at some sort of business. We couldn't afford to be here otherwise.

Me? A line of body shops and garages. You've probably seen them, maybe used one, but it's unlikely you'd connect them to

Ken Sasaki. I chose not to be the face of my company. Now that I'd sold it, I never would be.

We reached the crest of a low ridge and looked across the broader valley below. A cave could be made out in a cliff face, maybe a third of the way up the hill facing us. Our destination.

# 2.

THIS SIDE OF THE hill wasn't much different from the one we had climbed. Some different. It must be more sheltered, I decided. There were more trees, especially down low where a small stream bubbled through the valley. That would all be frozen in winter, I was sure.

Jad turned to Kat. "They will almost certainly name you Lu'ug, you know."

She smiled at that. "I expect it."

"Crow, right?" asked Bob. I didn't remember the word from my language lessons.

"Right. Any woman with black hair is called Lu'ug. We're not sure whether it is ever used for men." She gave Bob's long black hair a look. Maybe we'd find out.

"Isn't that confusing?" I asked. My own hair, despite my ancestry, was more a dark brown.

"It will be only one name. Most individuals have a long string of names attached to them," said Kat. "They keep adding them as they get older."

We started down the slope, slowly, and remaining as much in the open as possible. We didn't want to give the impression we were sneaking up on anyone.

"They'll see us in a moment," said Jad. "They always do."

\* \* \*

What we did here was harmless. All the experts agreed on that. Almost all the experts. And the hefty fee we paid helped fund research. Experts like that.

Below us was a group—a tribe, I suppose one could say—of lonely women. They would welcome a party of males if we showed any friendliness at all. There would be sex within a day or two. A good time would be had by all. Then we would leave them but it didn't matter. The general view was that the paradoxes involved would simply erase those days. It would be as if they never existed.

Or if, as Bob had suggested, an alternate time line was created, then they went on without any real harm. There might even be children. Or the tribe might disappear as it had in our own time line. We would never know. But we would not hurt anyone. There would be no rapes or mistreatment as had happened in some early tourist trips.

As Palit had suggested, we were driven by curiosity far more than by lust. We could not only see a world few others ever would but we were able to become part of it for a few days. There had never been anything like it in my lifetime and there never would be again.

The only thing that irked me was that we were not permitted to take pictures, or use any other modern devices. Only Palit and Chebab carried those.

I hoped Kat could be prevailed upon to share a few photos after we returned home.

* * *

"They've seen us," whispered Felipe. For some reason, we all felt the need to whisper right then, though no one at the cave could possibly hear our voices. Unless we shouted, and we weren't going to do that.

But there was shouting enough down below. "They'll scatter into the trees," Jad told us. "We won't go all the way to the cave but camp a little distance from it."

"Less likely to feel threatened if we don't trespass," said Felipe. "Right?"

Palit only nodded but Yukey said, "That's good common sense. Something we both should have showed from time to time in the past, huh?"

"You, anyway," replied Felipe. Both chuckled.

Had these two already known each other? I wasn't sure whether to say anything.

"Marquez and I go back," Yukey let us know. "Sometimes friends, sometime not."

"But always rivals. You know I'm going to get the best looking woman here, don't you?"

Ball only snorted.

"You'll find the women, ah, spread themselves around," said Jad. "Chances are you'll all have multiple partners. If you wish."

"They'll be as curious about you as you are about them," further explained Kat. "By the way, their men have gone missing for quite some time. That's why none will be pregnant."

"So we're entering a nest of horny, sex-deprived Neanderthal women," said Bob. "Sounds good to me."

"That's about it," agreed Jad. "And that is why this particular milieu is the one to which we keep returning. It's proven the most satisfying of any we've visited."

"And least dangerous," I had to add.

"Less dangerous, anyway. You could always be trampled by a mammoth."

I very much wanted to see a wooly mammoth. I knew they roamed much of Italy at that time. But anything large and primeval would do.

We were nearing the valley floor and stream. There was a fair amount of brush down here. Willows of some sort, hanging over the shallow, rapidly-flowing water. The ground beneath our feet was more pebbles than soil, and patches of dark green moss covered it here and there.

"Bare feet!" called out our leader. "No sensible Neanderthal would get his moccasins wet." Calling the pieces of leather wrapped and laced around our feet 'moccasins' might have been a stretch. "You'll find they all go barefoot in this weather anyway. You may wish to do the same."

We unlaced. I slipped my footwear into my pack, intending to go without the rest of the way. My fellow tourists carried theirs to the other side of the stream in their hands and there they slipped them back on. I suspect I was more used to going without.

Frogs. Not the first thing that comes to mind when thinking of Ice Age fauna. I wondered if our Neanderthals ate them. There wouldn't be much in the way of fish in this little brook. Damn, it was cold!

"Glacial run-off," said Palit. He pointed upstream. "We're not that far from permanent ice."

"Where do they get water in the winter?" asked Felipe.

Yukey snorted again. "Snow, you idiot."

"What do I know of snow? I grew up in Miami."

Ball snickered. "That depends on what kind of snow we're talking about."

Felipe only smiled and shrugged. I wished I'd researched my companions more thoroughly. Oh well, it was only for two weeks.

# 3.

I KNEW MORE ABOUT Bob. Robert Scoggins, novelist. Only super-ficially, to be sure. I'd even read his best-seller. Didn't like it at all but at least I didn't throw it across the room. I've been know to do that. My ex would admonish me about it, among other things.

We settled down at a spot maybe a hundred meters from the stream. The halfway point between water and cave. Half-ish. Bob started a fire from scratch. That's an admirable skill and one we were all supposed to have learned. Fire wood was scarce. Our Neanderthals might well have used most of it up in the area.

"Look to the stream," said Palit. "Some fresh wood should wash down it from time to time." So we went searching for drift-wood. Kat and I were one pair. She kept insisting on speaking to me in the Neanderthal dialect. I may have picked up a word or two from her.

"These may be the only people in the world who speak it," she informed me, dropping back into English. "An isolated tribe is likely to diverge rather quickly from whatever root tongue they spoke."

To which I could only say, "Then it's good we won't be running into anyone else." It had never happened before so it shouldn't happen this time.

"I wish we would," she said. "There are certainly other Nean-derthal tribes about. And—" She waved an arm to the south. "Across a narrow bit of sea our modern human ancestors may be camped." She remained quiet while we filled our arms with soggy twigs. "There is all of time to experience and we get a narrow two weeks."

"An experience most will never have. By the way, one of our new neighbors is up the bank a way, keeping an eye on us."

She didn't look. "Best we ignore her."

They would come to us when they were ready. That was the plan. We headed back to our site with what wood we had. Water might not be a problem in winter but what did these people use for fuel?

We had brought fresh meat with us. That was to be our introduction. Our bribe. Our packs—authentic animal skin sacks laced together with rawhide—carried a good supply of preserved foods too. Jerky, for the most part. Enough for our intended stay, enough to share and spread good will.

Steaks were grilling even now, the savory scent filling the air. That should bring in someone, if anything would. We added our wood to the pile Felipe and Yukey had started and seated ourselves on the grass. Even Jad crouched, tending the fire and cookery. We wanted to appear as nonthreatening as possible.

The first to show looked to be a boy. Mid-teens, maybe, and quite naked. "I think that's who was watching us," I whispered to Doctor Chebab.

Jad called out the word for 'friend.' Something like *pu\*cuc-cuc*, with the * being a click. There were a lot of clicks and whistles in the dialect. I thought it literally meant something more like 'harmless stranger.' The boy stared at us until someone called from concealment. He slipped back into the brush.

17

Our guide repeated his declaration of friendship and added 'food' to it. Or meat. My understanding was that there were a bewildering variety of terms that could mean food in all its forms.

Less than a minute later, a female appeared, an older woman. Matriarch was my first thought. I had no doubt she was the one who called the boy back. She was stocky, as was to be expected, but lean. She wore a hide skirt identical to Kat's.

Jad only waved an arm toward the grilling meat. Our guest hesitated but a moment before coming forward and hacking a chunk off with a heavy flint blade, and backing into the under-growth.

It was a first step.

* * *

The second step was for the entire tribe to appear. It didn't take long. I assumed the piece of beef was shared out and they voted to get more of it. Twenty individuals, exactly, including a baby at one of the women's breast. Five mature women—though a couple of those were barely mature—and the rest juveniles. The boy who had first showed himself was the oldest male.

I suspected he thought he was in charge. The alpha male. We would have to trust his mama to keep him in line.

The meat was shared out. They ate prodigiously. Feasted— that's a better word. It was good we packed in plenty, though we had all grumbled at being burdened with it. Some local produce, berries and tubers, was brought forth and shared with us. One of the girls tossed chunks of something brownish onto our dying fire. They caught flame and burned smokily.

"Dried dung," said Jad. "Reindeer, I would guess. The herds would have moved further north in this season."

"They talk a lot, don't they?" remarked Bob. I think we had all expected a more silent, stolid bunch. Why, I'm not sure. These Neanderthals chattered non-stop, once they got started. We tourists attempted a word or two, which was about all we knew. Some seemed puzzled we could not speak their language. The youngsters; the older women had undoubtedly run into other tribes in the past. One or two might even have been born to other tribes.

The others might not have realized other people existed. Neanderthal populations were sparse and scattered. So we had been told.

Jad was able to converse some. Kat even better, despite having learned what she knew of the dialect second-hand, via recordings. The women seemed to tolerate her but their eyes were on us guys.

Kat certainly noticed it. "You were told they would be interested in you, weren't you?" she said to us. "Isn't that why you're here?" There might have been at least a little sarcasm in her voice. So much for us not noticing she was there, as Palit had promised.

I was the one who answered first. "For me, it's an experience. An adventure, even."

"The sex is only a part of it," Bob said. "We get to—to *be* Neanderthals for a little while."

I think maybe all of us nodded agreement to that. Kat gave us a thin smile. "I do understand that motivation," she said. "In fact, if there were males around, I might even choose to experience the lifestyle the way you guys are going to."

I glanced at the biggest boy. Fifteen, maybe, if these folk aged similarly to us. He'd been looking at Kat more than a little. Staring might be more accurate. Best not to say anything about that!

It was getting toward dusk. At this latitude, at this time of year, there would be a fairly long twilight, a late setting sun. The matriarch stood and pointed toward their cave, addressing a rather long-winded speech to Jad. He said a few words back. I recognized enough of them to realize he was assenting to something.

He rose, as well. "We are invited to stay in their cave," he announced. "Our friend assures us there are wolves roaming in the night, as well as demons. If I understand the word properly."

We packed up and followed the tribe to their home. That was the third step.

* * *

I lose track of the steps after that. The cave was roomy, high-ceilinged. Peaked. The walls sloped in, like two smooth slabs of off-white stone leaning against each other. The mouth was partially closed up with rocks and other debris haphazardly heaped before it.

"We can assume they close it off completely when winter comes," said Palit. "As completely as they can. This cave has been explored in modern times. It does not extend deeply. No hidden chambers or anything of that sort."

That had been included in our materials. I had been a little disappointed to learn it. A deep mysterious cave where strange rituals took place would have been my choice. This was still wonderful, though. Every one of us could admit that.

Right now our hosts were dragging branches to fill up what opening remained. Maybe to keep out those wolves they had mentioned. Or the demons, for that matter. There was still some light outside.

Inside, a small dung-fueled fire burnt. Its heat was unneeded. All these bodies heated the place up almost too much. Did Neanderthals use fat-burning lamps of any sort? I couldn't remember ever seeing anything on the subject. There might not be enough fat available anyway. These folk needed all the calories they could get and were more likely to eat fat than burn it.

Some light would have been welcome, though. It would make no difference if we introduced any new technology to these people. When we were gone it would be as if it never happened.

I could look them over as they settled down to rest. More than a few had bulging tummies after we fed them. The youngsters— hmm, fifteen of them—varied in age and gender from the baby at its mother's breast right up to the boy who made first contact. They were a fairly robust bunch but certainly could have been better fed. Relatively light skins were universal. They all were well tanned at this time of year.

We remained separate for now. It would take a little while for enough trust to mingle. The children would probably be first. I turned my attention to their mothers. Five older women they were, though the youngest was certainly still in her teens. Maybe the youngest two. None would be considered old. Middle aged at most for our matriarch. What might have happened to any older individuals? Did they perish in the winter cold? Were they turned out when no longer useful? I had no way of knowing and not enough words to ask. It might not be politic anyway.

Two individuals went to sit beside the opening to the cave, spears in hand. A guard through the night. I'd be interested in seeing whether they worked out shifts somehow. It was one of the adult women and the oldest boy.

"Should we have someone stand guard too?" I asked the group. "To show we're going to be a part of the group?"

"That seems like a good idea," said Yukey. "Have the earlier visitors done that?"

Jad shook his head. "Not the first night. But why not?"

"I'll take the first shift. Wish I had a spear!" Yukey went to sit near the entrance but a little apart from the Neanderthal sentries. They glanced at him but didn't seem bothered by his presence.

Felipe whispered to me. "I suspect he will also keep an eye on the Neanderthals inside the cave. I know they were guaranteed friendly but I'm not inclined to be completely trustful."

And neither was Ball, nor myself, for that matter. I wondered if someone would wake me to take a shift as guard later, and slipped into sleep on a bed of fresh grass. It smelled rather good.

Certainly better than our hosts.

# 4.

I HAD NOT BEEN awakened. It seemed that Marquez took a second shift as sentry. In fact, he and Yukey were sitting together talking in low voices when I awoke. I wondered at once where I could pee.

And I was glad I hadn't felt the need during the night. Jad would know. Where was he?

There he was, coming from the darkness in the recesses of the cave. "I suspect you want the latrine," he said. "It's back there." He jabbed a thumb over his shoulder. "But you'll have to wait your turn. They are quite decorous about allowing one privacy in this, um, function, even if they do run about naked."

I wondered how they saw what they were doing back there. I'd probably step in someone's poop. Or fall into the latrine, if they dug one.

"Oh, and they are likely to have worms," he warned. "Pin worms, maybe hook worms—so be careful around their excrement."

"Won't they go outside soon?" I asked. It looked pretty dark still, what I could see through the small, brush-filled opening, but the mouth of the cave faced west. The rising sun wouldn't shine in.

"Eventually. That's up to Spruce Tree." Spruce Tree was the name the oldest woman went by, most of the time. There were a whole string of others that could be added onto it. I won't attempt to give any of them in her language.

I wandered back into the dark tunnel. The roof lowered as I

went. There were people waiting their turn. A prehistoric queue. They had them even then. One of the signs of incipient civilization.

By the time it was my turn my eyes had adjusted some to the dim conditions. It looked like our Neanderthals simply went as far back as they felt comfortable and performed their duty, in a spot strewn with leaves, small branches, dried grass. The ammonia reek was considerable. I'd not noticed it in the front.

But I would now. Maybe they cleared it out back there every now and again. They might even use the desiccated poop as fuel. We might not be around to find out and there were other questions I'd rather ask.

"There will be a breakfast soon," Kat informed me on my return. "It's a formal meal, with everyone getting their share."

A Neanderthal custom? Or something unique to this tribe, dealing with limited resources? That, also, we might never know. The meal consisted largely of meat left over from yesterdays feast. They didn't bother to reheat it, maybe to conserve fuel for the fire, which smoldered now, occasionally being fed a twig or two, or a dung chip.

That might have been a duty of the sentries as well.

Then Spruce Tree addressed us. Her voice was hesitant at times but she pushed on. The woman was unsure of us and unsure of herself, but doing her duty as leader. A duty that had fallen to her this past year.

"She is asking our intentions," explained Jad. He replied at some length. I could make out the gist of it. He was saying our people and her people would be one.

One until our two weeks came to an end. It was like playing a role in a play, knowing the curtain would fall, the actors go home. All the world is a stage, or at least this world.

Spruce Tree seemed satisfied. Pleased, perhaps. The other matrons of the tribe sat on either side of her. I hadn't learned their names yet. They were definitely pleased.

And I had no reason to feel guilty. I did, of course, a little. We would be making these people's lives better for a little lost bit of time. Then it would vanish. Evaporate as if it never were.

Spruce Tree gave the command to open the way to the outside. Dog Wolf took charge there. That was the oldest boy. Most of the tribe went off to do something or the other, but she and Jad sat and conversed longer. Some of it I could follow, some I could not. Kat or Jad tried to provide translations for us, now and then.

They were speaking of the missing men. I could tell that. Jad asked her how many they had been.

She held up one calloused finger on her right hand and one on the left. "Only two?" I wondered, not loudly.

"Five plus one," Kat explained. "These people count one to five on the left hand and then use the right hand to keep track of those fives."

Felipe laughed. "A human abacus! But what after they reach twenty-five?"

"Thirty," I said. "If they used both hands they could count to thirty."

He looked puzzled for only a moment. Maybe he was picturing the fingers in his head. "Oh, quite true, Ken. So what after they reach thirty?"

"They just say 'many many,'" Kat told us.

The woman went on at some length before Jad gave us any of it. "Four adults and a couple of teenage boys vanished, it seems. As the past times we visited. Her own mate, of course. And her brother. The biggest boy is her brother's son, or so he thought. Spruce Tree is not so sure."

This group was probably somewhat inbred. I wondered which was Dog Wolf's mother. Not either of the two youngest women, for certain. One of those did have black, or almost black, hair. I wondered if she was named Crow. Or if it was one of her names. The next to the youngest, a woman of twenty or so, I would guess.

Spruce Tree herself must be nearing forty. Her council with Jad at an end, she went outside. I think she intended to let him assign any duties to us.

First, he made an announcement. "I'll have to sleep with Spruce Tree tonight, as a symbol of our, um, tribes' union. That's the way it always works out."

"Only tonight?" asked Bob.

"We'll see. There are too many little variables in play to predict that sort of thing. I won't get in anyone's way as far as the other women go." I noted a faint smile from Kat but did not know the reason.

Four women, four travelers. After tonight, maybe five women.

In honesty, the sex part of this visit to the Paleolithic was being overshadowed by all the rest of it. There was so much more of this world to experience.

* * *

Today we were gatherers, not hunters. That should change. Felipe and Yukey chose again to go in each other's company so I ended up with Bob as my partner. I think Kat and Jad were making plans.

Not that we had to do anything our leader said. He couldn't send us back. That would happen automatically at the set time.

"I don't know how to be useful," Bob admitted.

"The only way to learn is to watch our hosts," I said.

"Oh, I don't mind watching them at all. Which, uh, which do you like?" He meant of the women, of course.

"All of them."

Thackeray's Barry Lyndon claimed he never saw such a thing as a plain woman. I'm inclined to agree with that. I didn't see any here. Ha, I wasn't going to find more attractive ones!

I wondered if Bob had read Thackeray. You don't know with young novelists today, even successful ones. He might not know the classics at all.

The women—no, none would be considered beautiful by the standards of our own world. But there was a beauty to them, a beauty that belonged to this time and place. Bob took a long look at the closest. "Yeah, I guess I agree with that."

I wondered if the women were having similar discussions. Whatever happened would be their choice, not ours.

So there was no point in thinking much about it. We'd have to get to know these people. Bob and I went down to where a group were busy at some task in the willows. Children, the littlest ones being watched by the slightly older, the oldest chopping at willow branches with flint edges. Digging into the roots, too.

At least half the tribe had hair of a reddish-brown. A dark auburn would be as good a description as any. Most heads were light on top, from exposure to long hours of sun. They were, as we had known they would be, a thick-bodied, large-boned bunch. Some, to be sure, more so than others. And they mostly had the rather large noses we'd also expected.

But they were, at worst, homely. There was nothing ugly or bestial about them. "They're all girls," whispered Bob. "Except the babies."

"Women's work, maybe?" Gender-specific roles had not been mentioned to us. Our instruction couldn't cover everything. "We should ask before intruding."

Not that it would make any difference. We could do no wrong here, really. If I didn't want to stick around, I could grab some of the supplies and go off to look for mammoths. Or anything else. We'd all be called back home at the same time.

I couldn't even die. Not really. I've mentioned that before.

Our fearless leaders came wandering down as we stood there. They, too, watched silently a little while.

Jad spoke. "I will be seen as the top male of our joined tribe. Our Neanderthals may expect direction from me. Also—" The pause was purposely dramatic, I think. There may have been a bit of a smile. "I'll be expected to lead a hunting party soon. Not that we need fresh meat or any food at all. We packed plenty enough in."

"How about a rabbit hunt to get our feet wet?" I suggested. I'd read enough to know the rabbit was a staple of the Neanderthal diet.

"Speaking of rabbits," said Bob, "do these people know how to set snares? Those willow roots they're gathering could make dandy snares."

"I'll go talk to them," said Kat, and headed away.

Jad watched her a moment before going on, perhaps making sure no trouble would come of her approaching the group of youngsters. "Rabbits, marmots, even voles," he said. "Anything small and furry they will hunt. They need all the food they can get, no matter what it comes from. Dog Wolf and a couple of the older boys are out looking for animals right now."

"Nothing larger?" I asked.

"The big game hunting methods of these people are suited to grown men."

"Running in and jabbing, right?" asked Bob. "Basically."

"Yes, basically. They managed to get a few reindeer when they passed through. Not enough. Last winter was a hard one for this tribe."

I'd read of the Neanderthal hunting technique for large animals. "They never throw their spears?"

"At smaller game. It's not so effective for the big animals. They can also be deadly accurate throwing rocks." He peered toward the young Neanderthals. "What is she up to?"

"It looks like she's joined them," said Bob. Sure enough, Kat was chopping away with a hand ax beside the kids.

"Why don't we reconnoiter?" I asked. "You know the lay of the land, Jad. Show us around, won't you?"

"Yeah, then you won't have to worry about us getting lost," Bob told him.

"We might as well," Jad said. So we did.

* * *

To be honest, we had all been provided maps of the area well before we came, though we were not permitted to carry them into the past. I'd studied mine pretty thoroughly. I can't speak for anyone else.

We headed south, up stream. Southeast really and that became more easterly as we followed the valley higher into the hills. Here and there it was joined by trickles from smaller valleys, some no more than gorges. We were somewhat distant from the peaks of the Apennines. "This water finds its way to the Tiber eventually," said Jad. "What will be the Tiber." He pointed toward the north. "Perugia would be up that direction."

"I would guess most of the reindeer migrate down the Tiber's valley," I said.

"That they do. It's likely only a few pass through here. Another herd travels closer to the coast, on the other side of the hills."

"And another along the Adriatic coast?" I hadn't read that but it seemed logical.

"We don't know," Jad admitted, "but I doubt any eastern herd goes as far south."

"A lot of the Adriatic would be dried up, wouldn't it?" Bob asked.

"Not as much as later. This is not the peak of the Ice Age." Palit turned toward the west. "Corsica and Sardinia would be one island out there in the Mediterranean, but there's a little water still between them and the mainland. Sicily would be connected." His smile was almost apologetic. "I'm no scientist, you know. I'm a tour guide."

A knowledgeable and highly competent one. "But there is a glacier up ahead," I said.

"Of sorts and a good distance yet. There is permanent ice and snow in the mountains but we're far from the sheet of continuous glaciation. It never reached this far south."

We trekked on a little further. It wasn't difficult across the grassy slopes. I kept my eyes open for game but saw nothing. That doesn't mean it wasn't there.

"Do you think we should have weapons?" Bob asked. "I mean other than the hand axes." We had all been equipped with replicas of those.

"Which you can use to cut and sharpen spears, if you wish," answered Jad. He had the only flint-tipped spear, which he carried now. There was no real expectation that the rest of us would seriously hunt.

"I'll keep my eyes open for suitable wood," Bob vowed.

What would make a nice straight spear shaft? "Hey, are there any spruces about? There must be or they wouldn't use it as a name."

"Further up the valley," said Jad.

# 5.

WE FOUND OUR STRAIGHT spruces, felling four small trees and roughly lopping off the branches. It was tedious work with a hand ax. We could smooth them this evening. Maybe. We might be kept busy with other tasks.

The sun was dropping. Jad held up one hand to call for a halt. "Something's coming this way," he half-whispered. We could hear it. A drumming, maybe, one could call the sound, coming from somewhere behind us, upstream. "Higher ground. Let's get some concealment."

We scrambled up the hillside to where brush grew along the base of a low outcropping, and crouched there. Almost as soon as we turned around to look, the first horses appeared. They were moving fast. Too fast to count but at least twenty. Running from something?

"There," said Bob, pointing. Smaller forms moving along the flanks of the herd. Wolves. They were not many. I'm not sure we saw more than five and that might have been the entire pack. They were attempting to separate a straggler from the rest of the rushing horses.

The horses were smallish, pony sized, and had bristling upright manes. Their coats were a uniform dun. Then came the unexpected—unexpected by the horses, unexpected by the wolves, and certainly unexpected by us. We should probably learn to expect the unexpected.

A tawny form charged into the herd, leaping upon one horse

that hesitated, unsure of its direction as the others scattered. In a moment, it was down, its neck in the jaws of a massive lion.

The wolves scattered too. They wanted nothing to do with this situation. The big cat looked about for a moment, perhaps making sure none would dare intrude on it and its kill, and then began to nonchalantly feed.

"That's something new," said Jad. "We knew lions existed in this time and place, but hadn't run into any before." He seemed decidedly pleased we had. "There's going to be more than a little envy when I take the pictures back." Our guide had a tiny camera strapped to him at all times. He undoubtedly shot a lot more footage than any of us realized.

"A male," said Bob, still peering intently toward the beast. "But without a mane."

"We knew they didn't grow much of one," Jad said.

"Not attached to a pride, I would guess," Bob went on. "Being a lone hunter."

Jad nodded. "And lone feeder. Wandered into the area on its own, possibly. Let's be glad there isn't a pride of them."

"Or hope there isn't a pride," I said. "And let us be thankful those horses were driven by or one of us might have been his meal."

"Yes, we would have walked right past his hiding place," said Jad.

We attempted to skirt the feeding lion as best we could. It is doubtful he would have bothered with us even if he saw us. His attention was on his meal. "I wonder if this will draw in any hyenas," Jad said. "I wouldn't mind getting some pictures of them too."

"As if wolves aren't bad enough," was all I had to say about that.

We managed to get back to the cave before the entrance was blocked.

* * *

"They say we should have washed," Jad informed us. "We stink a bit."

"You do," said Kat. "The rest of us went down and splashed some in the stream."

"Damn cold," Yukey added.

"It was," she agreed, "but the whole tribe seems to enjoy it. You've seen nothing till you've seen a dozen naked Neanderthals playing in the water."

"And it gave them their first chance to see us naked," said Yukey. "We all know they would have been curious."

Kat too? I suppose she would have joined in. Jad's only comment was, "I have no doubt our body odor is different enough from theirs to be noticeable."

Our hosts probably forgave our stench when Jad explained the reason. A lion in the neighborhood was big news. Some of them would have no idea what it was.

The tribe's hunting and gathering was meager this day and we hadn't even attempted any. We did have plenty of preserved meat to share. That was about the only sort of food we packed in— nutrition dense and palatable to these people.

"We should attempt hunting," said Jad. "Those who want to. You are all free to choose your own experiences here."

I piped up. "I want the whole experience and that includes hunting. I don't want to regret missing anything later."

"From the questionnaires you all filled out, it seems only you and Yukey have any experience at this sort of thing."

"I hunt every year," said Ball.

Felipe snickered. "I heard you just go into the woods in deer season and get drunk."

I had a feeling he might be right about that. I knew Yukey's type of hunter. Felipe's remark inspired the big man. "Say, do these people have alcohol?"

"Not that I've seen," said Jad. He gave Kat a questioning look.

"Fermented fruit *is* a possibility but it's never been documented."

"How about the stomach contents from reindeer?" asked Bob. "Isn't that sort of fermented? And I do know they eat it."

Yukey considered that but not for long. "Hmm, no thanks. I'm more the bourbon sort."

"Ah, but you haven't sampled Old Reindeer," Bob told him. He gave me a sidelong look. "That's part of the whole experience too."

"Except there aren't any reindeer around right now," said Jad. "We could go after one of those horses. And there are larger deer around. Maybe even giant elk."

"Shoot, why go after a giant elk when we can set our sights on a mammoth?" I joked.

But Kat answered seriously. "One mammoth could get this tribe through winter, pretty much."

If they exist after we're gone. There was no sense in saying that.

Instead I asked, "Who wants a spear shaft to work on?"

Bob and I each had one, and Jad didn't need another spear. Yukey picked one up without comment. "Not for me," said Felipe.

That left one. "Do you want it, Kat?" asked Bob.

She seemed to consider before shaking her head. She gave no reason.

Then I noted Dog Wolf looking at us. I looked back, straight at him, and held the shaft up. I pointed at it and then at him, and tried to look like I was asking a question. Neanderthal expressions were pretty much the same as ours.

I held it out to the boy, who came forward rather cockily—his friends were watching, after all. His whole tribe. He took the stave from me and began to turn away.

One of the women spoke rather sharply. The boy mumbled something I couldn't understand and left a little more subdued than he approached.

Kat snickered. "His mom told him to say 'thank you.'"

"That's Dusk Light," said Jad. "I think you just won her affections for the night."

The homeliest of the bunch was my first thought. My second thought was 'so what?' Dog Wolf was seated across the cave, examining the possible spear. He looked down its length, ran his hand along it. Then he began to scrape it with some tool.

We might as well do the same. If nothing else, we would have souvenirs to carry home. That was permitted.

# 6.

"WE PROBABLY WON'T ALL get laid tonight," whispered Felipe. "Some of those women will need time to act. Encouragement too."

I nodded, though I had no idea whether he was right. He had more experience with women, certainly. But not with Neanderthal women. Did all five of the mature women lose mates? There were only supposed to have been four adult men. The youngest was certainly a teen, but the others treated her as an equal. A matron of the tribe, which isn't really a very good description.

Hill Goat they called her. She might even be a virgin. We weren't going to ask. Or I wasn't going to ask. Jad probably knew. He'd seen earlier iterations of Hill Goat. He'd seen all these people.

In a year or two, had this tribe survived, Dog Wolf would have been old enough to be mate to one. Or all. Neanderthal polygamy? No one had brought the subject up. He was a large boy, standing as high as my shoulder, and certainly in his mid-teens but I suspected he had only recently reached puberty. Maybe that was typical of Neanderthals. Maybe it was a matter of this tribe's diet.

A mature Dog Wolf should be as tall as me. That's not saying a lot. I was the shortest of our group of travelers, not counting Kat. The other men were undoubtedly taller than any these people had ever seen.

I decided to follow the boy's example and work on smoothing

my spear shaft. It was pretty knobby; we had only lopped off the branches before bringing them back. I didn't think my hand ax was quite the appropriate tool but I could make a start with it.

The howling of wolves rose in the darkness outside. Distant. There would be sentries again, of course. Maybe none of us if we were otherwise occupied.

"Do you think the lion might show up?" asked Bob, of no one in particular. "I don't think that bit of brush and a few kids with sharp sticks would keep him out."

"I've considered that," said Jad. "The lion would have been here the other times this site has been visited, but it never showed itself. So, it is unlikely to now. We just happened onto to it when we traveled further away from here on this day than in the past."

"Unless it follows our spoor back here," I pointed out.

Felipe tried not to look alarmed. His voice came as a raspy whisper. "Do you think that is possible?"

"Possible but unlikely. Jad is right. Its hunting grounds are not near the cave." Not for these two weeks, anyway. After that, who could say?

I returned my attention to my length of spruce. It was a good length of spruce, eight foot or so, but it might be best to lop some off the smaller end. And thin down the bigger end, though that would be tedious. "Try this," said Kat, and handed me a smaller, thin flint tool, one better suited to scraping.

"Do you carry a complete Mousterian tool-kit?" I asked.

"As a matter of fact, I do. I learned how to make them myself."

She watched me make a couple passes with the sharp bit of stone. "That's what we call a Levallois flake."

"The peak of Neanderthal technology."

"So-called early modern humans are making Mousterian-like tools in North Africa and the Near East right now. Our ancestors may not have been as separated from the Neanderthals as some believe."

Some of the tribe gathered around to observe me at my task. There were murmurs but I couldn't make any words out. None that I understood.

"They're noticing the flake you're using. They haven't had any new stone tools in a while." Kat exchanged a few somewhat halting words with them before saying, "None has the skill for tool-making. That knowledge went with the men they lost."

She spoke with them again. There were frowns and what sounded like words of disagreement. "Ah, they feel it is men's work. Some were appalled when I offered to teach what I know."

"Not all?" I ran the blade along the shaft again. It was looking better but the light would soon be too dim to continue.

"There are those who will place practicality over taboo," Kat replied. I wondered which but didn't ask. It probably would not matter any. "We learn new things of them each time a party visits. It makes a great laboratory. That's one reason we keep coming back. Just the money you guys give us wouldn't be enough."

"It's getting too dark," I said, putting my work aside. The fire

41

gave only a little light and these folk, as I'd noted before, had no lamps. I was still thinking I could do something about that.

Two youngsters crouched near the entry, our sentries. One was Dog Wolf, still working on his spear shaft. Everyone was settling down. Darkness would have to provide any privacy. It was too warm to cover up with a hide.

Jad slipped away. Should I approach someone? It was getting too dim to know whom I might be approaching! That would work the other way too. All four of us seemed hesitant, even the usually self-confident Yukey. I decided to act. That consisted of standing up, stepping forward, and looking around. A voice called softly, with a bit of a question to it.

I went to answer that question.

* * *

I didn't know how my fellow tourists fared nor did I intend to ask. It was indeed Dog Wolf's mother, Dusk Light, who had invited me to her bed. It proved a surprisingly comfortable bed of grasses, much better than those we had made for ourselves. It smelled rather nice. I suspected the woman had gathered fresh grass early, in anticipation.

Whatever she anticipated, I hoped I lived up to it. Dusk Light herself was a clumsy lover but an eager one. What opportunity would a woman in a small isolated tribe have to learn much of such skills? Not that I was greatly experienced. I had one wife to whom I had been faithful, and there had been no one since we split. I think maybe that split was what made me seek out a new experience, something completely different from my usual ordered life. My rut.

I kind of wished I could talk with her. I did learn a few new words, or inferred what they probably meant, in the course of the night. Words I might not use anywhere else. We became tired enough to halt after a while but not too tired to resume when she woke later and shook me awake. She was quite insistent.

I slipped away when we finished that time, first to use the back of the cave and then to sit with the sentries. Children again, but not the same ones. One was an older girl, maybe twelve or so. She began to chatter at me. Never mind that I couldn't understand much of it. I did catch the word for 'mother' several times. She seemed to be making a point of using it.

I caught on. "Dusk Light mother?"

The two whistles of differing pitches I knew to mean 'yes.' My first real conversation with a Neanderthal. So this girl was Dog Wolf's little sister.

"Ken," I said, pointing to myself and then to her. Like a Tarzan movie.

She giggled and replied, "Rabbit." In her own language, of course. That was a name of youth, the name of a girl. She'd get more mature ones later on.

Rabbit had a wealth of freckles and was a rather cute little girl, and not just for a Neanderthal. She didn't take after her mother much and didn't look a whole lot like Dog Wolf either. I remembered that Spruce Tree had doubts about the boy's father. This girl was presumably her niece, the daughter of her brother. I could see maybe something of Spruce Tree in her.

A little more food and they would all look better. Even Dusk Light.

Kat came from the gloom and peered out through the tangle of brush in the entrance. "Still dark out?" She turned an ear to the opening and listened for a moment. "Raining. Pretty hard too. I guess I'll just sit here with you."

She then spoke with Rabbit a bit in the girl's language. Kat suddenly burst out laughing. "It seems Dog Wolf has decided I am going to be his wife. He is certain Great Bear has sent me."

Rabbit seemed amused by it too. But I wouldn't have been at all surprised to hear that she had designs on one of us.

"Oh, here come our other two satisfied customers," said Kat, as Bob and Jad approached. "The Yukster and Felipe didn't get any last night."

"They will," Jad said, taking a seat beside us. "Last Star and Hill Goat are still shy of us."

"But She Bear practically dragged me away," said Bob.

"I'm not surprised. She's the most likely to sample all of you. Or attempt to."

Bob might have looked slightly disappointed. But after all, she chose him first. Well, yeah, Jad and I were already taken.

"She named me Ra'ara. I don't know what it means."

"I don't think I've heard that one before."

"I've seen a similar word in reports on another dialect," said Kat. "I believe it means Raven."

Jad nodded. "So a man with black hair is liable to be called Raven, just as a woman is dubbed Crow."

"Perhaps. We shouldn't assume too much. Hmm, Ra'ara. You're recording this?"

"Of course. I record everything."

None of us was going to ask him if that included last night. We surely all wondered though. It must have showed.

"Yes, last night too, not that it was interesting. It never is. Spruce Tree's not necessarily that impressed with me. Sex was a formality, a symbol of joining our tribes. If she seeks a partner tonight, it is unlikely to be me."

He might have sounded a little relieved about that. I wondered if Jad went out of his way *not* to impress the Neanderthals' leader. How many times had he gone through this scenario anyway? Not a great number, I knew, but at least three or four times before.

"People are stirring," said Kat. "Let's do the same."

* * *

Rain continued to fall, a soaking rain, sometimes wind-driven, sometimes coming straight down like a heavy, gray curtain.

"The climate is not much like the Italy we know," said Jad. "There is no great Sahara Desert in this period, sending its hot winds our way."

Most of us huddled in the cave. A couple of the more brash youngsters briefly went out into the downpour.

Jad looked over our group. "I have to officially call role twice while we're here. Regulations. This seems like a good time to get it out of the way, with you all together. Euclid Ball?"

45

"Yo."

"Katherine Chebab?" Oh, he had an alphabetical list.

"That's *Doctor* Katherine Chebab," she answered.

"With a diploma from a university that doesn't exist yet," observed Bob.

"Felipe Marquez?"

"Don't know where he is," Felipe claimed. "I'm G**. Rabbit named me that."

Jad had no comment. "Ken Sasaki?"

"Here," I responded.

"And Robert Scoggins."

"I want to be a doctor too," he stated. "My alma mater *did* bestow an honorary degree on me. Do our Neanderthal friends have shamans or witch doctors or something of that sort?"

"Not enough of them for that sort of specialist, is there, Kat? Everyone has to be their own shaman. Okay, I won't need to call roll again until just before we leave. Let's hope you're all still here."

"Do you know what G** means?" Kat asked Felipe.

"Not the slightest. The girl couldn't begin to pronounce Felipe so she just told me who I was."

"Egg, right?" asked Jad.

"Egg in a Nest, to be precise. Probably because of your head, Felipe."

He patted his bald dome, fringed with dark untidy hair. "I've been called worse. Egg in a Nest is okay. Or Nest Egg. I like that."

Yukey snickered. "They should've let you bring your toupee."

Spruce Tree was organizing something or attempting to. Jad felt it was his duty to go and find out what. "They're going to clean out the latrine," he reported on his return.

"But you already knew that, didn't you?" Bob asked.

"I did. It always rains this day and they always use it for that purpose."

Yes, I thought, the rain always came but the human dynamic changed with each group of visitors. They could have chosen a different way of spending the morning.

"We are allowed and probably expected to help," Jad went on. "It's not gender-specific work, even if the women are using their digging sticks."

All the women had digging sticks they carried about with them much of the time. Now pretty much everyone able had a stick and was pushing the litter in the back of the cave into a more compact pile. "Muc!" Dusk Light called out. Spruce Tree gave her an annoyed look.

Usurping her authority. I'd already figured out that was part of the dynamic here. I couldn't figure what a 'muc' was, however. It turned out to be something between a net and a basket, made of loosely woven bark-string. It looked more like a hammock than anything else. Rabbit and Dog Wolf had brought it from some-where up front, and now laid it on the cave floor while others used their sticks to push some of the litter onto it.

"Here's where we can help," I said to whoever was listening. Yukey was the one who caught on and came to help me lift the filled muc and carry it forward. "Where?" I asked. I had to say it in English, I'm afraid. My Neanderthal remained at somewhere between minimal and nonexistent.

But Rabbit caught on and led the way. I had kind of assumed it would go out the cave's mouth, but no. She stopped beside the hearth. "They're gonna burn it," said Yukey.

I figured he was right. Throwing their waste out the front would probably attract unwelcome visitors, so not only excrement but gnawed bones and other garbage ended up in the back of the cave. A lot of it was grass. We dumped it and returned for another load.

Dog Wolf, incidentally, was holding onto my side to help out. He was quite possibly every bit as strong as me. About halfway along, She Bear had decided to assist Yukey and she stuck with him for the several more needed trips. I could make a pretty good guess who would share her bed tonight.

As we finished up, some swept the space with branches or scattered handfuls of sand about. Armfuls of dried grass were carried back and deposited. "Old bedding material," commented Jed. "It's an excuse to replace the grass. Gets rid of vermin too."

I assumed they had fresh grass ready at hand. It wasn't the best of days to go out and gather more. Spruce Tree had gone forward and was beginning to feed the fire from the pile of trash beside the hearth. This was one day a large fire would be welcome.

"Come look at this," said Bob, at my elbow. "This is the way to make a bed."

Several were at work on this task, though not all were choosing to change their bedding this day. We watched Last Star.

I think maybe Bob liked to watch Last Star. She was perhaps twenty or so, with black hair. To no one's surprise, Crow was one of her names. She was also Spruce Tree's daughter.

Under the grasses lay a packed layer of ash. "That beats putting it directly on rock," I said. "Or even sand."

Bob nodded. "It does. Maybe I'll have a chance to report on how comfortable it is."

I could only laugh at that. "I'm going to go sit by the fire," I told him. "I know that will be comfortable."

# 7.

IT WOULD BE A good day to try to learn the language. I might never get beyond the names of a few things, I knew, and it didn't really matter. "Having some Neanderthal words will be another experience," I told the others. "One we can take back with us, so to speak."

I grinned to make sure they caught the pun but they ignored it anyway. It was also a day for crafts. Bob began to mess about with some of the willow branches and roots, working on constructing a couple snares. He had apparently studied up on the subject before coming. Not something I would have thought of. A group of youngsters watched him. I doubt they had any idea what he was making.

I watched a while too. "What is that tool you have there?" I asked.

He held it up. "Clam shell. Sharpens easily but doesn't hold its edge long. I don't know enough to ask where they got it, but there are more of them."

"That might be useful for finishing off our spears." Maybe I should get back to work on mine. But there were more interesting things going on. The muc lay beside the hearth, where Spruce Tree continued to sedately feed the flames. Of what sort of fiber was it made? Bark, it looked, twisted into ropes. Not braided though.

I glanced up to see Spruce Tree looking at me. She turned her eyes away quickly. The woman had a tough job here, leading this remnant of a tribe. It was not a job for which she seemed suited but she was doing her best.

Whether that best was enough, who could say? I didn't think she was the sort to take chances, and chances might be necessary for their survival. They needed to leave this cave, maybe. It wasn't too late for that, only the beginning of summer.

I wished I were able to speak with her. Instead, I only smiled and went to work on my own piece of spruce tree. Kat was seated beside it and with her was Dog Wolf. She was showing him how to work a piece of flint.

"Hey," she said, "Dog Wolf says they have several chunks of raw flint. No one knew quite what to do with them." She gestured toward an array of objects spread beside here, stone, wood, bone. "They had the proper tool set but its owner is gone."

She held up what looked to be a piece of antler. "Hand axes can be worked more finely with hammers like this. More important he learn how to fracture useful flakes from the core."

Important? Nothing we did here was important. She was teaching a ghost. Dog Wolf would vanish. Evaporate.

Maybe. There was always that alternate timeline theory. We'd never learn whether there was anything to it. I put my back against the cave wall and smoothed my brand-new soon-to-be spear.

* * *

Apparently, I fell asleep.

Rabbit was squatting on her haunches, looking at me, when

my eyes opened. My spear lay across my lap. Kat sort of snickered when she asked something.

"She wonders about your eyes," she explained.

"I sometimes wonder about them myself." I stretched and rubbed those eyes. "Can't you make up a good story?"

Kat thought for a moment and then spoke to the girl. Rabbit broke out into laughter. "Bo*ca! Bo*ca!" She jumped up and ran off to share the joke.

"I told her you were part lynx. I'm afraid that might be your name now."

"I could do worse. It beats Egg Head."

"Egg in a Nest. And yes, I would say it is preferable. Your parents came from Japan?"

"Grandparents. I'm third generation, raised in small-town Tennessee."

"Oh, so that's where you got that accent." She'd probably read up on me but I didn't say anything about it.

As I've mentioned, my hair is naturally a dark brown. It even has a bit of reddish tinge to it when I'm out in the sunlight—not so different from some of these Neanderthals. The idea that everyone Asian has black hair is just a stereotype.

But no one would take me for anything but Asian, otherwise. "My dad opened a garage in a country town and I kind of built it into a chain when I took over."

"And sold it."

"Yeah, I was tired of not having a life." My wife got tired of it too. "Where did Dog Wolf go?"

"Outside, I think. The rain's let up and Bob the Raven wanted to set his snares." Her slight smile suggested an amused tolerance. "He studied up on them before coming. I don't think he has any practical knowledge."

"I'd say he's the sort to throw himself into things. He learned more of the language beforehand than the rest of us." He'd taken all of it more seriously than the rest of us.

"Maybe it's like writing one of his books for him. Immersing himself."

That seemed entirely likely. It also seemed likely Robert Scoggins would write a book about Neanderthals when we returned. Maybe a novel, maybe not. I'd be willing to read it. I had no idea how I would fill my time otherwise. The future was a blank.

"The women wondered why I'm not involved with one of you guys," said Kat. "I told them I was Jad's mate."

"What does Jad think of that?"

"I'll find out when I tell him. He should approve. It gives us both a plausible reason to remain separate."

I took to working on my spear again. "I guess I'll have to make do with a sharpened end. I suppose you know how to attach a flint head." Like the weapon Jad carried.

"In theory. Some Neanderthals used a sort of glue they made from birch trees. And fiber binding, of course."

"Hmm. I guess I'll make do with the pointed stick approach. I could try making a spear thrower."

"Not used by these people. Not in the form you're suggesting, for heavy shafts like that." Kat nodded toward my piece of wood.

"It doesn't matter."

"No, I suppose it doesn't." She laughed. "But don't get any ideas about bows and arrows!"

"Aren't they inventing those in South Africa right around now?"

"But they won't reach here for another forty thousand years. I'm surprised you know this stuff."

"Bob's not the only one who can research."

It would be something like twenty thousand years before the atlatl, the spear thrower, would show up here, carried by modern humans. But I'd read that Neanderthals and maybe even the Heidelberg humans who preceded them had used throwers for some sort of light darts. Throwers could be used for rocks, too.

None of that mattered, either. I did decide to keep an eye open for birch trees.

\* \* \*

"No one told me about this."

Everyone was singing. There was no discernible continuous tune; each singer seemed to go off her own direction as her turn came. They might just be improvising the words too.

Yet they were tuneful. Tuneful enough. Rhythmic, not so much. I hadn't learned near as much of the language as I had hoped today. I shouldn't have taken that nap! Very little of it could I follow but they seemed to be telling a story. About someone named Tall Deer Mountain Pine? Maybe he was one of the missing tribesmen. Maybe he was a figure from legend.

All the women laughed as She Bear's tune went off on a

strange flight. She laughed good-naturedly with them as Dusk Light took up the lead in the huskiest voice of the group.

Yukey leaned over and said, not quite whispering, "I'll be with that She Bear tonight, I'm fairly sure."

To which Bob said, "I suspect we'll all change partners. A game of musical beds."

That seemed to be to everyone's approval. The woman were as curious about us as we were about them. Things would settle down in a while. Then we'd be gone.

Many of the tribe, young and old alike, were streaked with paint, or colored clay. I think it was just mud on the smaller children, in emulation of their elders. Plenty of mud available outside today. Jewelry had also come out, bits of bone, a few sea shells on leather thongs or willow-bark string. These seemed to be treasures and were not worn most of the time.

I wondered if men sang at these affairs. Kat and Jed were sitting off to the side so I couldn't ask. Nor could I ask Kat if she intended to join in. She did not look eager to be noticed at all. Neither did Jad. They were getting out of our way. We, the paying customers.

The fire was dying down. Grass only burned a short while. Howling arose outside, closer than I'd heard before. Spruce Tree rose at once to give orders. Some of the older children hurried to finish closing off the cave mouth with brush.

The entertainment portion of the evening had concluded. My spear was more or less ready, sharpened at its tip, though the shaft could be further smoothed. I picked it up. "I'll sit with the first watch," I announced.

Dog Wolf was already seated by the entrance. Maybe I could practice Neanderthal on him. One of the girls, maybe ten or so, joined us. She had a sharpened stick, just like me. I hoped she knew how to use it.

The cave fell into darkness, only the dim light of the coals making one little warm island in the dark sea of night. Feeding that flame was one of our tasks, we who watched. The three of us conversed in low voices as the rest of the tribe became silent. Mostly the children spoke. I tried to learn, asking what I could now and again.

But I kept an eye out for what was going on with my fellow travelers. Kat and Jad had found a bed away from the others, where they could play at their charade of being mates. Yukey slipped away almost at once. I knew where he was headed, as did everyone else. Where Bob went, I couldn't make out but he did not return.

And Dusk Light came and got Felipe herself. The pair disappeared in the direction of her bed, the bed I had visited last night. I admittedly had taken myself out of the running tonight by volunteering for sentry duty. I was willing to let the others sort things out. After what must have been two or three hours, Dog Wolf sent the little girl away. "Wake up watchers," I think was the explanation he attempted to give me. Sure enough, a couple minutes later Rabbit and Hill Goat showed up to take our places. I chose to sit and talk a little while first and Dog Wolf remained. I don't know whether he actually wanted to but he was following my lead.

If Hill Goat was not with someone, then Bob was sharing the bed of either Last Star or Spruce Tree. I strongly suspected the former, considering the attention he had showed her earlier.

A few minutes later, Spruce Tree came out of the dark. Hesitant, she seemed, but she held out a broad hand to me. "Come?" Why not? I thought, and went with her into the night.

# 8.

"ONE THING YOU SHOULD recognize," said Jad, "is that it might be possible to contract some disease from a wild creature. That won't matter in the long run but it could ruin the remainder of your stay here."

Bob shrugged. "Another experience."

It was one experience I wouldn't want. We were all in quarantine a while before traveling back in time, and would be again on return, though some of the scientists believed it impossible for any germs to return with us—that it would create too much of a paradox. The authorities preferred to be careful anyway.

These people had been in an effective quarantine themselves, having had no contact outside their group in a year. If by chance they did contract something we carried, it shouldn't matter, right? Not after our two weeks had passed.

It was to be our first hunt, bright and early this fourth day in the past. Wolf Dog—and about every boy in the cave and some of the girls—had wanted to come along but we informed him he had to guard the cave in our absence. In truth, we just didn't want him to observe our ineptitude. Maybe if we got a little better!

Also, the boy was put in charge of the one rabbit Bob had actually managed to snare last night. Carrying that back to the cave would be as triumphal an entry as any.

"I'll find new spots and reset them this evening," said our long-haired author. I think he felt like having his own triumphal entry.

"What are you gonna hunt with, Egg?" asked Yukey. The rest of had spears.

"This," replied Felipe, holding up a thick branch. "If anything gets close enough, I'll club it."

Felipe knew nothing of hunting. None of them did, really, but Jad had gotten a little experience on these trips into the past. Euclid, as mentioned, had done some shooting but knew little of the woods. I did. I was not a country boy exactly but I'd spent a lot of time outdoors.

They might not all want to hunt the next time around but were willing to try it out today. Eager, even.

"Downstream?" asked Jad.

"Good a direction as another," Yukey answered. None of us saw a reason to disagree. If nothing else, we'd have an interesting walk around the neighborhood. I do think all of us liked the idea of carrying something back to the cave and the women. However small. There was no real reason to want to impress them but we were guys and pretty conventional in that respect.

"You know the women are probably sitting around comparing us right now," said Bob, as we made our way along a grassy slope.

"The sample isn't big enough yet," Felipe told him. "More testing will be necessary."

I had other things on my mind. At the moment. "If we go higher we might spot something," I said. "How about going up this ridge a little?"

"Or we might even surprise a marmot sunning itself," Jad said, and turned up the slope without further words.

A brush-filled gully lay in our path a short way up. "We can go up and around there," said Bob pointing. The others started away, but I stood looking the bushes over.

"Hazelnuts. This would be a good food source in a few months." I turned toward my companions. "The tribe should be told of it if they don't know."

"But they won't actually be here," Jad reminded me.

"Maybe, maybe not," said Bob. "We don't know, really, do we?"

I realized I was beginning to think like Bob. Perhaps these people did go on in their own timeline after we left. Perhaps our actions did matter. Or maybe it was no more than wishful thinking. I did not at all like the idea of them vanishing, now that I was coming to know them. Now that they had become real.

Below us lay the stream, wide and shallow, its margins hidden by the scrubby willows. "Do you know if there are any birches around?" I asked Jad.

"I wouldn't recognize them if I saw them," he replied. "Any reason why?"

"They're a resource to these people too." According to Kat. "The bark." I looked toward the top of the ridge, where pines rose here and there above low outcroppings. "Those might be too. Pine nuts." And their resin might be useful. I didn't know enough.

I did know a few pine boughs—or spruce for that matter—might be a nice addition to the bedding back in the cave. Just grass got smelly pretty quickly. It was too absorbent.

"Hey, we're hunting, not gathering," said Yukey.

Bob looked up. "There might be eggs to gather on some of those cliffs."

Jad scanned them. "Pigeons. They do nest on the ledges but I don't know if this is the right time of year."

"What is that at the bottom of the cliff?" Bob shielded his eyes from the sun, trying to make it out. I certainly couldn't. We climbed further, until we stood at the base of the low escarpment. What he had spied seemed to be a small cave.

I turned and surveyed the landscape below us. "There's some forest down further," I said. Maybe those birches could be found there. Maybe oaks. Acorns were a food source. I wanted to go look but I turned my attention back to our hole in the ground.

"It's rank," said Felipe.

"Maybe a bear dens in there. Or even our neighborhood lion," suggested Bob.

I took a whiff. "Or a polecat."

"A skunk?" asked Yukey, backing away a little.

"No, a ferret. Want to take a look inside?"

"Not without a torch," Jad decided. "Let's move on."

But I did intend to get a look in there. And maybe at the forest and the cliffs and the pine trees. I was beginning to feel we did not have nearly enough time.

* * *

"There are no musk oxen this far south," said Jad. "I much doubt we would see a wooly rhino either."

"But maybe a mammoth?" I still very much wanted to glimpse one.

"Maybe. This *is* near the southern edge of the wooly mammoth's range."

Chances were they had moved north for the summer. Much of the large game might have. It was the price we paid for visiting during good weather.

"Maybe we'll see those horses again," said Bob. "We might even be able to spear one."

Yukey squinted at the younger man. "You'd be willing to eat horse, Bob?"

"Why not? I've had worse. And call me Raven," he said. "I want to be Neanderthal till we go back to our boring lives."

"Sounds good to me. Then I'm Lynx," I told them.

Jad chuckled. "Kat gave me the story on that. So shall we move on down toward the river?"

River it could be called, maybe. More rivulets had added to its flow. It was still far from large. We all grunted approval or nodded, and set off down the slope. I could hear Felipe mumbling something about needing a better name.

"Hold!" I hissed, raising a hand. I'd spied something, over to our right. "That might be a marmot," I said, pointing.

Bob—I mean Raven—shook his head. "I think it's too large."

Maybe so. I set off in its direction and the others followed. I hoped to circle above whatever creature it was. Sneak up on it.

"That's a bear," said Jad, when we were about halfway there. "A good-sized cub."

I think every one of us knew what that implied. I began scanning the slopes for a mother. While backing away. We were all backing away. Of a sudden, a towering figure rose out of the deep heather near the cub, its head turning back and forth as if searching.

"Down!" ordered Jad. I doubted Mother Bear could pick us out by sight but her nose might be more accurate. Regardless, best to be as inconspicuous as possible.

But I couldn't help thinking here was more meat for the tribe. Warm furs, as well. Could a fat bear be killed come fall? What was I thinking of? I'd be long gone from here. If 'here' still existed.

And I certainly wasn't ready to tackle a bear hunt right now. We crawled away from the pair. Mother dropped to all fours, apparently losing interest.

"The famous Cave Bear?" asked Yukey.

"A bear is a bear is a bear," answered Raven. "I think it will kill you just as dead whatever you call it."

We made our way to the bottom of the valley, not rising from a crouch until we stood by the stream. Something unseen bounded away. Something edible, perhaps.

A deeper pool lay before us, shaded by tall trees. Not the scrubby willows that grew near the cave. From their bark, I was fairly sure some were the birch I had asked about. A different species from what I had known at home.

"I wouldn't be surprised if there were some decent-sized fish in there," spoke Felipe. "I need a rod, not a spear."

"That we could make," I said. "Or at least a hand line of some sort. We'll have to come back and try it sometime." I pictured myself tying some sort of primitive fly. "Oh. What do we do for hooks?"

"Shell is best," said Jad. "Maybe bone or antler. I think something could even be made of wood that would serve in a pinch."

"Or we could try spearing a fish," Raven added. "What do you think? Trout? Char?"

Something cried out above us, a rattling call. Felipe identified it at once. "Kingfisher. I can't pick it out." He scanned the branches above the water.

"So we know there are some sort of fish in here," I said. "A deep pool like this could be home to a pike or two." It lay still before us, the trees reflected in its dark surface. Yes, I could imagine a big pike lurking somewhere in its depths.

"At least we don't have to worry about Ice Age alligators," joked Raven.

That was true. It would always be pretty safe to go into the water here. Cold but safe.

* * *

It was just the season for the ripening of blackberries so we didn't return to the cave empty-handed. We filled every pouch we had with the fruit. We also sported more than a few wounds from our encounter with their thorns.

I couldn't help worrying that our bears might come down and join us. There were certainly suspicious tracks but they were too muddled to be certain of them. Especially after my companions trampled the area.

The sun was sliding toward the horizon before we got back.

Dog Wolf met us on the trail, carrying Raven's snares. Eager to reset them, and with ideas for better spots. The boy might have been thinking of them all day. After a few words exchanged, mostly with Jad, the pair went off to attend to the chore.

Our berries would not begin to feed the tribe this night, nor the rabbit Dog Wolf had carried home. We travelers didn't care about that. We had plenty of what we had brought still in reserve. I think we would have liked to be seen as successful hunters, though. There's nothing wrong with wanting to impress the Neanderthal women. Any Neanderthal guy would want to!

I might say things to the effect that these Neanderthal women were thickly built and big-boned but they were no more so than women I knew in my own time. Some of them relatives. Anyway, they were women and I found none of them unattractive. Or unattractive enough to be a problem. Ha, that sounds crass, doesn't it? Better to just say I liked them all. It would be the truth.

Still, they all tended to have deep rib-cages and short limbs. Of course, there were also the relatively low, long heads. Pretty big heads. Late-period Neanderthals, on average, had bigger brains than we modern sorts. They were not stupid by any means. There were the relatively heavy brows but, again, I've seen ones as heavy in Tennessee. The chins were not prominent—or non-existent—but the sturdy jaws made up for that.

And they all had those big noses. I'm not sure whether Dusk Light or She Bear had the largest honker. They looked a bit alike. I figured they were related, but then all of the tribe was related.

The women were waiting to greet us before the cave. If they were disappointed, they didn't show it.

Indeed, they were delighted with the fruit and carried on discussing it for some time. The friction between Spruce Tree and Dusk Light seemed to flare up a little again. Dusk Light had what was surely an 'I told you so' attitude going on.

Kat explained it as we went inside. "They have been cautious about going that far afield," she said. "They are very much aware they might run into a bear, and have no one there to protect them. Dusk Light has suggested they carry spears themselves and chance it but Spruce Tree has always vetoed her. The rest have been willing to follow her so far." The woman snickered. "And now they have men so the problem is solved."

I hoped they would find the confidence to forage further from home when we were gone. Or even leave the home and find a more hospitable spot to winter. Maybe that was why the tribe disappeared. Maybe they went to live on the seashore.

Our snare-setters returned, some of the brush gate was put into place—the gap would be filled completely later—and the evening meal began to be set out. This included our berries, piled on a large flat stone, some of our dried meat, and, to be sure, a grilled rabbit.

Yukey grabbed a handful of the berries. He had big hands so it was quite a few. Felipe beat the rest of us in admonishing him. Maybe we were a little reticent to cause any problems. That didn't seem to bother the Egg. "We ate enough of those when we were picking them," he said. "Leave them for the women and kids."

The big guy considered this and let most of them fall back. A few did find his mouth. I don't think he felt the least guilty.

A knot of children were giggling and peeking at him. The women also seemed to be having an amused discussion. "What's with them?" he asked.

Kat informed him. "They are arguing over whether you should be named Fat Bear or Fat Marmot. Fat, either way."

"Hey, I'm not that fat." He truly looked offended. Maybe he had been dieting.

"These folks haven't seen anyone as heavy as you in a long time. Maybe never. And they consider it a compliment. It means you have been a successful hunter."

"Oh. Well, I hope they go with Bear."

I suspected I would think of Yukey as Fat Marmot from now on.

It is to be noted that there was no side-by-side woman and man seating yet, aside from Kat and Jad. No one felt attached enough to share mealtime. Not so with sex, I guessed. Who would be with whom tonight?

That question didn't apply to me. There was no mistaking that She Bear had chosen me as her partner. She couldn't have been more obvious if she'd hit me over the head with a club and dragged me away by the hair. I very much assumed she intended to try all of us on for fit. Maybe more than once. It had been good with Spruce Tree last night. Good enough. I could have settled in with her for the rest of our stay and I think we both would have been okay with it.

Maybe someone low key and steady just appealed to me right now. We were about the same age, I figured.

The light began to fade. She Bear looked impatient. I'd let someone else watch at the cave mouth tonight.

# 9.

SUCCESS HAD BECOME FAILURE with the snares. When Raven and Dog Wolf checked them in the dawn light, they found that something had torn apart and eaten most of the one rabbit they had caught.

"Dog Boy says a fox, as far as I can make out. Probably right."

He stood gnawing a piece of cold meat. Felipe and I were pretty much finished with our own breakfasts. Someone would suggest a course of action for the day, sooner or later. I didn't care. I think yesterday's long hike had worn all of us out.

"I was that odd man out they talk about, last night," said Felipe. "Bob and I both, um, made ourselves available to Hill Goat but she was having none of it. He ended up with Dusk Light, I'm pretty sure—" He looked up at Bob Raven, who nodded. "And Yukey with Last Star. Spruce Tree didn't want anything to do with any of us."

"Ken spoiled her," said Bob.

"Wore her out," I corrected him. At once, I felt stupid for having said it. But I didn't retract the statement. Nor was I going to make any comment on my own night. She Bear's kids kept interrupting, including her taking a break to nurse the youngest.

But I talked more with her than any of these Neanderthal women so far. A few more words in my vocabulary, for what that was worth, and even a little history—very recent history—of the tribe. I comprehended enough to learn she was Dusk Light's kid sister, and that her own mate had come to them from another tribe. He couldn't speak a word of their dialect when he arrived.

Never once did she mention his name.

Yukey was late to join us. He seemed in a foul mood. We pretty much ignored him when Kat and Jad appeared.

"I suggest we take it easy today," spoke our fearless leader. "Wander if you wish, or loaf in the cave. We'll work up another expedition in a day or two." He paused. "If you want."

Felipe and I gave him agreeable nods. Yukey grunted. "Dog Wolf and I are going to go off and look around together, then," said our Raven. "Maybe even attempt some small game hunting."

I was tempted to do something of the same sort, but I was sore. Especially my feet. I decided to go down to the stream, perhaps wash up a little, and take it from there. Maybe I'd try making a fishing line and hooks later. We had passed a tree with large thorns yesterday. Maybe those could be used as part of a hook.

No, I have no idea what sort of tree it was, being both Ice Age and European. That didn't keep me from sawing off three of the thorns with my hand ax.

Birch bark. Native Americans used that to make string for fishing lines. I'd read that somewhere. Was it mentioned in *Hiawatha*? I'd identified a little with him as a kid, and First Nations culture in general, looking different from all those around me. Anyway, willow bark would undoubtedly work. Or even willow roots, as they were.

I sat on one of the higher sandy banks watching the water. Best to let the air warm up a little more before I went in myself. There were insects dancing along the rippled surface. Hey, I could catch some and use them for bait, perhaps. Or if I found some feathers, I could make flies of a sort. These Neanderthals liked feathers and each had a few among their treasures. Even the little ones.

Someone or something approached from my left, largely obscured by the drooping willow branches. Not a bear! Too small. Kat emerged into the sunlight.

"Mind if I sit?"

"Go ahead. It's a good morning for it."

"It is." She sat quietly for less than a minute before saying, "You come across as, um, the most capable and level-headed of us all. Aside from Jad."

This was obviously leading to something. "Is there some sort of trouble?"

"Maybe. I sat and talked with the girls, I mean the tribal matrons, after you men left this morning. They've sort of accepted me as one of them, even if I don't have any ritual scarring."

This was something I had noticed on all the women. The five matrons, as Kat had referred to them. "Is that part of an initiation into womanhood?"

"It is, but that's a different subject. Oh, but they do expect you guys to have an initiation ceremony for Dog Wolf now you're here. There haven't been any men to attend to it."

And these men would be gone. Maybe we could do something before we went. Had previous expeditions to this time and place bothered with it?

"Of course, the girls talk about you all," she continued. "Including how you are in bed. They're pretty candid about it."

"I won't ask for my report card."

"Don't worry. You've passed. But Ball was so worn out last night he fell asleep early. Then he woke up in the wee hours and wanted to have sex but Last Star didn't and he may have overstepped hospitality. This is something Jad needs to sort out."

"I'd sort him out good," I said.

"Any of you guys would. Best to leave it to him. Jad has total authority, as you know if you read everything you signed."

"My lawyer did."

"Then you know he could execute you out of hand if he wished and you could do nothing about it."

"Because I wouldn't really be dead. I'd leave a dead body here but I would appear back in our own time."

"Guides like Palit are chosen as much for their mental stability and sound judgment as anything else. He would be extremely unlikely to abuse his authority. He'll give our Marmot a talking to."

I watched water flow for a little while. "And do our women have any thoughts on all this?"

"As usual, Spruce Tree counsels restraint and Dusk Light wants to beat him with a club. I promised to have you guys take care of things."

"Passing the buck." I might have liked to see five Neanderthal women belabor Yukey a little. "Someone's coming."

She looked back into the willows, the way she had come. "No, up the stream." There was a figure wading toward us. "Hill Goat."

"Not hurrying. Hmm, I think I'm inhibiting her from

approaching." She turned and gave me a serious appraisal. "Approaching you." Kat stood and slipped away into the bushes.

The young woman was still slow to come toward me. She pretended to be looking elsewhere for a while, before turning to me and saying, "I greet you, Lynx." In her language. I knew enough to translate that.

"I greet you, Hill Goat." I hoped I said it right. It was an exceptionally complex language and what was right coming from her mouth might be completely wrong coming from me seconds later. "Sit?"

I reached down and gave her an arm up, to take a seat at my side. Hill Goat was the most deeply tanned of all the women. Her thick bush of wavy hair, hanging in natural dreadlocks, looked almost blond from the bleaching of the sun. And unlike all the others, there was not a freckle in sight.

She began a narrative of which I could only make out an occasional word. Then tears came. I hadn't seen anyone cry here but there was no reason they shouldn't. Hill Goat leaned against me and sobbed, before straightening up again and resuming her mystifying story. When she finished, she leaned back just a little and looked at me, as if she expected some reaction.

I figured sympathy and concern would be a good place to start. That went well—I mean, she did smile—so I held out my arms. She embraced me for but a moment. "Swim," she said. Not exactly swim. One didn't swim in this shallow stream. The words meant more like 'play in the water.' Hill Goat doffed her kilt and lowered herself to stand in the ankle-deep flow over a gravel bar.

I decided to do the same.

* * *

Quite some time later, we lay side by side, hidden by the deep grass. The sun was moving toward its zenith.

I rolled over on one elbow to look at Hill Goat. She needed a better name. Maybe I'd think of one. "Cave?"

She blinked both eyes, which was one of several ways her people signaled assent. We rose and slid on our hide skirts. Hers had drilled and polished pebbles attached around the waist, on rawhide thongs. Something moved in the grass, off to the east. It was being stealthy. I pointed it out to the girl.

"Wolf."

Yeah, she was right. It moved to where I could briefly glimpse its gray coat. Where one wolf was, there might be a pack. I had left my spear in the cave and carried only a hand ax.

"We'll bluff our way through," I told her, though she understood not a word. "Like this." I took off the kilt I had just donned and held it over my head, waving it back and forth, both arms outstretched to make me look as large and threatening as possible. Hill Goat caught on at once and emulated me. We advanced on the wolf, howling and shrieking.

Its nerve broke. It turned and loped away into the grass. Hill Goat giggled and then hugged me. We both took off running for the shelter of the cave.

We did stop before getting there to put our clothes back on.

* * *

I don't know whether Hill Goat embellished her story but she certainly dramatized it. She had to give it to anyone who would listen as soon as we got back. I hoped she left out the adults-only parts. Children were there, after all.

And those children worried me. Where one wolf showed up, others could follow. I didn't like the idea of a child running into them, no matter how many or few they were. I needed to tell someone this, but wasn't sure how. I supposed it would have to go through Jad or Kat. Or both.

I didn't see Jad around. He could be up to anything, anywhere. Hmm, none of the guys were in the cave. Only Kat.

"I take it things went swimmingly with Hill Goat," she said as I approached, and then snickered at her own witticism. She held up a tiny modern-day device. "I admit to recording her long-winded tale. It proved to be pretty much the story of last winter and how her mate had disappeared and her mother had died. I think the father must have already perished at some point. And how she was alone and the other women were mean to her and she didn't like the other men who came with you but she thought you were swell. I guess she demonstrated that, but you got too far away for the microphone I'd hidden to pick it up!"

Her mate. I had found that Hill Goat was not a virgin. That had relieved me some, not that I could have done anything about it had I discovered otherwise.

"In other words," continued Kat, "she went on like the teenaged girl she is. But she's also a woman, an adult in a world where one has no choice but to grow up."

"I suppose I gave permission to eavesdrop in the contracts I signed."

"You bet. I also get your first-born." She was on a roll.

We sat down by the cave wall, away from the fuss around the girl.

"Where is everyone?"

"Bob, uh, Raven, is out with the tweens again, doing the hunting and gathering bit. The others went for a walk. I think Jad and Eggy wanted to have a talk with the Marmot."

"Okay. I want to get everyone on the alert about the wolves in the neighborhood."

"You could order the tribe around anyway you wanted right now. You're the hero, the alpha male, in pretty much all their eyes." She snickered yet again. "Yet here you are, the runt of the litter."

"You probably know something about that yourself."

"Don't I! It sucks being short."

"So I'd best assert myself while I've a window of opportunity."

"A very small one. In at least some respects, these people have a matriarchal society."

"I can understand that," I said. "The men go on long hunting expeditions, leaving the women to run things."

"That's a good theory. Or maybe women are just superior."

"As long as they don't beat their husbands."

She got serious. The scientist in her, I reckon. "There is no formal marriage among them nor any kind of ceremony. A couple simply chooses to be together and that bond can be broken by either at any time. If there are children, they are more likely to remain together."

"I would hope so."

Kat shrugged. "The tribe takes care of the kids more than the father does. In fact, I believe there are six orphans among the children right now. Last Star helps care for them more than any. Her child died and she has none of her own now."

In time, everyone found their way back to the cave. Raven's minions had an assortment of unappetizing-looking roots and seeds and small animals. I didn't ask about Yukey. That was no longer my business. My own tale was spread about—or Hill Goat's story. There was continuing discussion of wolves and the need to carry spears and so on. These people definitely didn't formally debate anything. They just gabbed and gabbed and sometimes even sang, and seemed to reach some sort of conclusion.

And when it came time for our evening meal, Hill Goat sat down at my side.

"She's claiming you as her mate," said Jad, in a matter-of-fact voice.

Kat said, "You can move away from her if you wish. It would hurt her feelings but it wouldn't kill her."

"And maybe she'd show interest in one of us, then," added Raven.

I stayed put.

# 10.

THE THING IS, HAVING a mate was a valid part of the Neanderthal experience. Much better than sleeping with a different woman each night. That lost its charm after the third night. So the fourth night and maybe every night we remained, there was Hill Goat.

Then she would be gone or I would be gone or whatever.

I couldn't decide whether the Goat was the most attractive or the ugliest of the women. Both simultaneously, perhaps. I mean actually ugly, not the ordinary homeliness of the others. Deep-set blue-gray eyes peered from beneath the heaviest brows among the women, made to appear even more protruding by the thick, almost shaggy, eyebrows. She Bear and Dusk Light appeared to have almost no eyebrows at all, ones so pale they were barely noticeable.

Striking may be the word I want. Otherwise, her face was fairly regular. Almost a younger, slightly finer version of Spruce Tree's visage. They were cousins of some sort. Maybe cousins of more that one sort, considering the inevitable inbreeding that went on.

Her slim, lithe body lay beside me in the dark. Was any life really better than this one? Were we any happier sixty thousand years from now?

I didn't want to go back.

But I would. I had no choice. There would be an automatic return two weeks after arrival. That was set when we were sent back in time. The device that sent us could be destroyed and it would make no difference.

It is true any traveler will pop back on their own sooner or later anyway. No one had managed to stay in the past more than twenty-two days, we were told. It was probably the truth.

As no one can stay very long, it puts a crimp on research because everything is 'reset' when they visit again. This makes it hard to run a long term study.

I would get up soon. This could be a day to experiment. I had worked on fishing gear yesterday afternoon but I needed more there. Maybe more than I could accomplish in my time here. And there was Dog Wolf. We could give him his initiation, yes, make him a man in his eyes and those of his tribe, but more importantly he could be showed the sources of food they needed for survival. Hill Goat, too. They were their people's future.

I could barely make out her form. She was what? Four years older than the boy, at most? In a couple years they could be a couple and I would be only a fading memory for Hill Goat.

And Hill Goat and all these people a memory for me. One I expected I would treasure for whatever life I had left. The sixth day was upon me. I should not waste it.

* * *

Felipe—I just couldn't bring myself to call him Egg—chose to come with me this morning. We did have our fishing lines. Hooks, too. Felipe had painstakingly shaped a couple from a small bit of bone. I'd used my thorns, tying them at an angle to twigs with bark string and daubing the joint liberally with resin. I think it was pine, not birch. Dusk Light had a gob of it among her possessions. She was a bit of jackdaw in that respect.

I didn't know if we would find time to use any of our 'tackle.' There was much else to explore. In particular, I wanted to look over that little cave we had found. Even if a whole tribe of ferrets inhabited it. The sun was barely over the hilltops when we arrived. We knew the way now and had made straight for it. "Why the hurry?" groused Felipe.

I could have explained how our limited time here had weighed on me, made me feel a need for urgency. "Why waste time?" was as good an answer as any.

The entrance was certainly large enough for a man to enter, if he slid in. I wouldn't do that without a look first. We'd brought torches for that, and an ember from the fire, packed in dirt inside a skin bag. We shook it out onto the ground now and got a blaze going from twigs and grass. The torches were the ends we had trimmed off our spruce trunks. They should burn well but maybe not long.

I got one burning and thrust it into the hole. "It's a real cave," I reported. "Not just a hole under a rock." That was just what I had feared it might be, no more than an animal den dug back under the rock. But it opened wide almost at once into a small, globe-like chamber. "Um, I seem to have been wrong with the polecat theory," I added. "The place is full of bats."

"I hope they eat these damn mosquitoes."

I backed out. Some of the dirt could be shoveled away from the entry but it was not essential. "Here. Light up." I held out my torch. A few seconds later, I descended into the cave feet first,

Felipe behind me. There was a little slope down to the irregular, bowl-shaped floor.

"Bats indeed," noted Felipe, holding his light up to view the ceiling. The floor was plastered with their droppings, appearing yellowish from the little circles of light our torches cast.

"Watch your step," I warned. "It's likely to be slippery."

He nodded. "There's no standing water. It must drain somewhere."

True enough. "You know something of caves?"

"Not really. That's just true of any hole in the ground, isn't it?"

"There's air flow too. Our torches are flickering. Ah, and there is a low area down the center with no guano. It must be washed away regularly."

Felipe looked up again. "A little bit of water dripping there right now. Filtering down through the rocks."

"I suppose so. This is almost as much a sink hole as a cave, you know?"

"That it is. There's the way into another space." He gestured toward a darker place on the wall with his torch. The only slightly damp stream bed led into it. "I do not think I would want to live in this cave."

Neither did I, but I could see it as a refuge, if needed. The next chamber was on a lower level and much larger.

"A cathedral!" breathed Felipe, holding his flame above his head. The ceiling was high, too high in places to see by the illumination of our torches. Stalactites and stalagmites had formed, joining to create opalescent columns in places. I was a bit

81

surprised a bear or other large carnivore hadn't made this its den. Maybe one did in the winter.

"I think it may continue beyond," I said. "I wouldn't chance going further with these quick-burning torches."

"Me neither. Let's get out."

That proved a little more difficult than anticipated when we reached the entry. The rock slope was a bit slippery. If I came back, no, when I came back, a ladder of some sort might be handy. A rope at least. With a bit of shoving and pulling of each other, we managed to once again stand on the grassy slope outside.

"A cathedral," I murmured, almost to myself. "The perfect place for Dog Wolf's manhood initiation."

"Ha, you think like a priest, Ken. Shall we try fishing now?"

* * *

We sat beside the pool. Felipe had improvised a short rod from a piece of branch. I just dangled my hand line over the edge of a rock. Bait? We'd brought along some guts from the small animals that made up part of last night's meal.

"You and Jad had some words with Yukey, I understand." I had been reticent to bring the subject up at all, but this seemed a good time to see how things stood.

"We did. I think we made him see reason."

"Reason?"

"Reason. What will make our stay here go most smoothly. It's no good to appeal to the man's better side. He doesn't have one."

A pause, as if he wasn't sure whether to enlarge on that. "Believe me, I know."

"You've known him a while."

"More than a while. Nearly twenty years of dealing with each other, off and on. Sometimes as competitors, sometimes as partners. Hey, a nibble. Nope, didn't take it. Anyway, Ball and I both broke a lot of laws on our way up. The difference is I knew I was a—well, criminal. At least sort of. Yukey felt he was entitled to do what he wanted. I'm sure he never thought of any of it as being wrong." He lifted an empty hook from the water and scowled at it. "I'm not entirely sure he knows the difference between right and wrong."

A bit of a psychopath, I thought. The sort that lives a fairly normal and sometimes quite successful life. There were more of them than most folks realized.

"Give me another piece of mouse gut, will you? Thanks." He impaled it on his hook and lowered the bait into the still water. "I left the illegal activities behind long ago. Most of them! One can make plenty of profit legitimately. But Yukey would suggest various schemes to cheat, almost every time we did business. I got the feeling he just liked putting one over on people. Outwitting them to inflate his own ego."

Maybe more a narcissist than a psychopath. "Yet you continued to do business with him."

"Forewarned, forearmed, Ken. I knew he couldn't be trusted— not to deal honorably, not to pay if he could avoid it." His chuckle didn't sound particularly mirthful. "Watch him complain when we return to our time, and demand a refund. *All*-right!" He lifted a small silver wriggling form clear of the water. "Hmm, char, I think. I've caught 'em in Canada."

He looked toward where the stream flowed out of the pond. "I'd probably catch more of these if I went over there to the shallower water."

"I'm after the big pike I know is down there," I told him. "Sleeping in the depths."

"The char taste better." He went a way down the bank to cast. By the time we wound things up he had two more char. I had nothing except a sheaf of birch bark. I had stripped it from a couple of the trees with my ax when we arrived.

Maybe the stuff would be useful.

# 11.

KAT KNEW ABOUT BIRCH tar production. That was why I knew to gather the bark. I'd had no idea and if left to my own might have tried to tap the tree somehow. "Chance are," she told me, "Neanderthals simply burnt birch bark in their hearths and scraped the tar off the rocks later. At least at first."

"You mean accidentally?"

"Uh-huh. That's probably how they discovered it. Then they learned to do it on purpose with larger flat rocks around the burning bark. Like a chimney. But it's better to heat it up in an enclosure rather than burning it directly." She shook her head. "They may never have figured that out."

"Like making charcoal," I said.

"Just so. What one gets is sort of an oil. It can be reduced further by heating."

"Well, I think we're going to introduce our tribe to a new technology."

"Might as well. I've been instructing Dog Wolf in an old technology. He's picking up flint work pretty well."

I was working on another technology as well, my spear thrower. Maybe I could fasten a stone head to my spear, with the birch tar as glue. Oh. "Where do they get their flint?" I asked.

"The men seemed to have brought it from somewhere. No one can agree whether they found a source or traded for it."

Figuring that out would be beyond the scope of our limited stay here. We'd have to hope the tribe found a source eventually.

If there was a tribe. No, Ken, there's no need to think that way, I told myself. Assume they will continue when you are gone.

"Maybe we'll save the bark for tomorrow. I guess we need to break out more dried meat. Three little fish aren't going to go far for supper."

"It's time the menfolk went on another hunting expedition."

"Yep, if we can tear them away from the womenfolk."

"The women boycotted all sex last night, as a retaliation for Yukey's indiscretion. You may not have noticed, being kept busy."

No, I hadn't noticed and Felipe had said nothing of it to me. "I guess I had good timing getting married."

She smirked. "Somebody did."

"Reckon things are smoothed over now?" Everyone seemed amicable at the moment.

"Sure. They'll be back at it tonight, have no doubt. Um—" She glanced toward a clump of Neanderthal women. "Spruce Tree says she will sleep with our Fat Marmot tonight, to sort of bring him back into the tribe, symbolically. Not that she used that word. She may not be a genius but she has an understanding of that sort of thing."

I'd rather have seen Dusk Light thrash him with a club but didn't say that aloud.

"And She Bear has her sights on Egg Head. Then she'll have tried all of you on for size."

"Think she'll make a choice then?"

"I don't think any of them feel there is a hurry. Unlike Hill

Goat. Oh, they are calling her Wolf Chaser now. The name might stick."

"I could claim that name," I said. "In a masculine form."

Kat shook her head. "I'm afraid I've saddled you permanently with Lynx."

That wasn't so bad. I wished I could still use it when I went home.

* * *

I heard laughter in the darkness.

"You two are waking everyone up," came Jad's voice.

"Yeah, get a room!" Kat added.

Maybe Goat and I had gotten a little noisy. I attempted to translate for her. I don't know if her giggles were over their comments or my mangled Neanderthalese.

At least we could converse a little and not just because I'd learned some of her language. The young woman had picked up some English words she'd heard us using. Rabbit had too. She let me know now that she wanted to return to lovemaking. We didn't really need words for that.

I pulled her to me, her taut body, her firm breasts—hmm, firm is too much of a cliché, isn't it? Sorry, I didn't have a thesaurus with me. Maybe Bob knows a better word. Go ask him and leave us alone, okay?

Bob? With Dusk Light tonight. Last Star wasn't interested.

Many energetic minutes later, Hill Goat slept. I decided to rise and take sentry duty. There was no schedule for this. At least not one of which I was aware. Individuals were awakened and they took their turns. I would let someone else sleep for a while. Dog Wolf was still on guard when I reached the entry. He always seemed to take the first watch.

And he took the duty seriously. He greeted me gravely and told the little girl watching with him to run off to her bed.

She was a year or two younger than Rabbit, and generally called Acorn. There was a boy about her age and the rest of the children ranged down to She Bear's baby, less than a year of age.

That next oldest boy after Dog Wolf was not the sharpest flint flake in the pouch, to coin a Paleolithic phrase. They named him Nut Grass.

Nut grass, incidentally, was a part of their diet. The tubers or roots or whatever—I guess nuts is as good as word as any—could be gathered readily enough through this relatively short season of warmth and growth.

But Nut Grass the boy would never rival Dog Wolf. Not as craftsman, not as a leader. As a hunter he was unlikely to be more than another spear-jabber. Healthy spear-jabbers could be useful, especially for defending the cave. The man he would grow into should not be a liability to the tribe.

And Nut Grass was a presentable little fellow. Our Dog-boy was considerably homelier. He looked much more ungainly than he was, with his thick body and short, heavy limbs.

I had brought my spear and was polishing it with a piece of rough-grained rock. Sandstone, I'm fairly sure—the replacement for sandpaper. It was not local but was among the tools left behind by this tribe's vanished males.

I cursed softly when a splinter found its way into a finger. Dog Wolf held up a hand for quiet, while craning his head toward the cave's mouth. I listened. A snuffling. Something pushing its way into the piled brush. My first thought was the lion but that thought left me just as quickly. A lion wouldn't sound like that.

A dark snout appeared. A bear. Dog Wolf stood his ground, holding his own spear before him.

When it comes to bears, I had a lot more experience than the boy. He would never have actually interacted with one before. Probably not. I put down my spear, picked up a small, springy branch, and swatted the beast across the snout. It whined and backed out. I could hear it half-sliding down the slope before the cave.

I realized it could have gone an entirely different way. An angered bear could have pushed on in. But it seemed to want in anyway, so why not take the chance? I wasn't going to second guess myself now, especially after my bluff worked.

Half the tribe seemed to have awakened. Dog Wolf regaled them with a tale of my prowess. And his own courage, too, to be sure. I put a hand on his shoulder in approval.

But to my time traveling companions, I said, "A youngster, probably in its second summer. Maybe recently parted from Mama and looking about. I figured it would be easy to spook." A full-grown confident boar could have been quite another matter. I hoped one of them never investigated the cave. They'd probably have more sense than to go poking their noses in, though.

# WHEN MAN WAS YOUNG

*  *  *

It seemed that Hill Goat and Lynx would be, respectively, Wolf Chaser and Bear Chaser, at least for a while. The Chasers—a nice Neanderthal couple.

We would hunt today, and it seemed only right to take Dog Wolf along. Felipe chose to remain behind. "Someone needs to protect the women," he claimed. Despite the jesting tone, I did trust him with that job. The women, to be sure, might need some protecting from Felipe.

"Let's head off that way," suggested Yukey, pointing toward the higher hills that rose behind the cave. "We haven't looked that area over yet."

We climbed across the ridge, a bit south of the cave, and surveyed the inhospitable valley beyond. It was narrow but not deep, with steep, rocky sides. It grew even steeper at the bottom, practically a ravine, where a trickle of a stream flowed south. It probably joined the stream we knew at some point. Beyond, far beyond, rose the pale violet-blue of mountains, fading into the morning sky. Not high mountains, I was sure. The Apennines lay off that way; perhaps those were part of them or maybe they were only hills that led to the main attraction. I wished I had a map with me, but I did remember a spur of the higher country wrapped into the region south of the cave. Well south, I thought.

We had descended the more gentle higher slope and begun to pick our way downward into the gorge when Dog Wolf touched my elbow and pointed. Something moved along a low escarpment opposite us. I peered at it a moment, trying to make it out. "I believe that might be a chamois," I said. "Something similar, anyway. It doesn't look like a goat."

A goat would have been just as good though. Plenty of meat on either animal.

"How do we get to it?" asked Jad. "Even if we were good spear throwers, it's too far away."

"If the angle were a little better, we might be able to knock it down with a rock," suggest Yukey. "It would need to move down a little further."

Instead, it moved up, picking its way along what seemed a sheer rock face. It paid no attention to us. I've no doubt it knew we were there but too far away to seem a danger.

"I might attempt a cast," I said, my voice quite low. I wished I had more than a pointed stick. The flint spear head was still something for the future. In fact, Kat might be distilling the birch tar for it right now. The tip of my spear had been hardened in fire. That would have to do.

And I had my spear thrower. I'd completed it, practiced some with it, yesterday afternoon. Accuracy was definitely not a guarantee, and this was a longer cast than most I had attempted. The chamois was almost directly opposite us now. I'd not get a better chance at it.

After all, what did I have to lose? Back went the arm, balancing spear and thrower, the fingertips of my left hand barely touching the shaft to steady it. The body was poised more or less sideways to my target, ready to pivot off my front leg. I made very certain I had enough room and wouldn't be tumbling down the steep hillside!

In other words, I looked like a pitcher winding up for a big overhand fastball. Because that was pretty much what I was throwing. No waiting for signals. Transfer my weight forward and let fly, the arm snapping straight. The atlatl did slip out of my hand but the spear flew true, hitting the unsuspecting chamois behind the shoulder. It cartwheeled toward the valley floor. Hitting bottom killed it if my projectile didn't.

"Well, I'll be damned," said Yukey.

Dog Wolf jumped up and down from excitement and then bounded down the steep way to the carcass. We followed more carefully. Fortunately, my spear thrower was in plain sight. I wouldn't need to make another.

Though I certainly should, as a backup. Or for the boy to use. Would it work as well with his body shape?

We roughly butchered the animal. Dog Wolf wanted to keep more of the entrails than we would have thought to. By noon we had it back to the cave. The woman were critical of how we had mangled the creature's hide but none of us cared.

My name from now on was Spear Thrower. Spear Thrower Bear Chaser Lynx. But soon the tribe went back to just calling me Lynx.

# 12.

HALF OUR TIME HERE was gone. I was a satisfied customer, so far, but wanted to make the most of what remained.

We feasted on chamois that night. One small antelope didn't really go that far for twenty-six of us, although some stomachs were smaller than others. Make that twenty-five. She Bear's baby lived on milk alone.

I spent the evening fastening a flint spear head to my now-blooded weapon with many wrappings of bark string and the newly-made birch tar. At once, Dog Wolf wanted the same for himself.

"You must make a suitable flint head yourself," Kat told him. "Then we will help you fix it to a spear shaft." I actually under-stood enough of her words to get the gist of that.

But I didn't think she was the proper translator to speak to the boy of a manhood ritual. I hoped I could depend on Jad for that. We should attend to that in the next couple days. I also wanted to make another foray north, to gather more bark, to fish again, to maybe get a look at the forest. The stream turned more westerly there, flowing down toward the wide valley of the Tiber. Or what would be the Tiber.

I'd kind of like to see what sort of river flowed there now. No time for it. But that shorter jaunt, for sure, whether any of my fellow tourists wanted to come or not. I did want to bring one or two of the younger Neanderthals along, to show them what resources were available. Ha, they were my tribe. I had to take care of them.

I suggested an early start. No one seemed very interested. I couldn't even get Dog Wolf to come. It seemed he and Bob were back to their snares.

"I'll come with you," offered Kat. "I don't need to sit around this cave anymore. I'll tell the women."

No sooner had she done so than my Wolf Chaser stepped forward and directed a long and seemingly slightly miffed speech my direction. I got that she wanted to come too and thought I should have invited her first. Maybe I should have.

Rabbit jumped up. "Me too!" Or words to that effect.

"Hmm, tell her she has to keep up or we'll leave her behind for the wolves."

There was a slight widening of the eyes but I don't think the girl really believed me. "I'd best come along too," spoke Felipe. "Shoot, they might end up protecting me but I'd feel better about it."

"And you can fish again."

"There is that."

So it was decided. I took early watch that night. Hill Goat Wolf Chaser was sleeping when I found my bed a few hours later. Best to let her slumber, be rested for tomorrow. Me too. I hadn't paid any attention to who was bedding with whom tonight. It interested me less now. Knowing who shared my own bed was enough.

If only for a week longer.

* * *

We would go nowhere near our cavern. That would be for

another time. We did skirt some low cliffs along our route, however. It was easier walking higher along the heather-clad slopes than close to the stream.

Again we noted pigeons coming and going from ledges. Hill Goat was for climbing up and looking at the nests. "Later," I told her. "On the way back." I think that's what I told her.

I wondered if it would be possible to climb up in the night and nab the birds themselves. Not worth the danger. Not unless one were very hungry. Hmm, maybe nets.

We did not turn aside to the pond. I wanted to look at the woods; they really started around the area of the pond and extended downstream, growing wider, taller, thicker. Oaks, to be sure, with acorns coming on them. These I pointed out. It wasn't too far to come and gather them, I said.

Hill Goat answered at some length. "They know," translated Kat. "They didn't have men to come along and protect them last year. Though—" She nodded as the girl went on. "Dusk Light wanted to chance it anyway."

There were thickets of hazelnuts too, as I'd seen before. I'd pointed those out as we went past them. Maybe the Neanderthals already knew of those also but it didn't hurt. Rabbit was rather wide-eyed in the forest. She had not been here before and spent much time looking up into the trees, where squirrels scrambled and chattered as we passed. Small ones with tufted ears, they were. I've shot a few squirrels in my time, yeah, and ate them too. There was no way of knocking these ones down. I'd leave them to the real lynx that undoubtedly roamed these wilds.

Or martens or owls or whatever other hunters might be out there. I suddenly felt a little vulnerable among these trees, with these women for whom I was responsible. Something larger squalled, not so far away.

Hill Goat was proud to show off her knowledge by giving us the beast's name. Unfortunately, we did not know what it meant. It was a new word for Kat. After some questioning, she nodded. "I think it's a leopard from her description. Not very dangerous to us. Fairly small and related to the Clouded Leopard of our time."

"I think it's time to turn around anyway," I stated. "Hey, that's a walnut. That would be worth coming here for on its own." I looked around. Sun dappled the ground here and there, breaking through the leaves. It really was a rather nice, open bit of forest.

"I'd rather live here than in a cave," I said.

"Until the wolves ran you up a tree," said Felipe. "You fishing?"

"I'll leave my friend Old Pike to his dreams today. We'll just splash around and spook everything in the pond."

He gave me a disgusted look. "Better chances of catching something a little below it anyway. The stream widens out just a tad below the outflow. A good spot—if I had my split-bamboo rod and a selection of flies!"

When we reached the water I did fish for a few minutes, having brought a line, and my companions being interested. Felipe went downstream as promised. It was nearing noon, and a better day for napping than much else. I dangled my hook over the bank and lay back.

"Shall we eat?" asked Kat. "I packed a regular picnic."

"A picnic of dried meat? I shoulda picked what you packed." I sat up. "I'd rather get in the water first." With that, I dropped my kilt and jumped in. My, that was cold! I knew I was at a deep spot and it had been safe to take a plunge. I paddled about a little.

Rabbit and Hill Goat were agog. "I don't think they've ever seen swimming before," said Kat. "They've only splashed in shallow water."

It was then that Rabbit decided to join me and jumped into the water. She sank of course. I heard Hill Goat's scream. The first time I'd heard any of the Neanderthals scream. I pulled the struggling girl to the surface, sputtering and coughing. "Don't fight," Kat called out to her. "Lynx has you."

I don't know if Rabbit heard that but she did relax. I kicked over to the far edge where her feet could touch bottom.

"What the hell happened?" called Felipe, thrashing his way through the shallows at the far end of the pool. "I heard a god-awful screech!"

"Rabbit thought she could swim," Kat called to him. "Turned out she couldn't."

Felipe looked at the girl and broke into guffaws. Rabbit even giggled a little herself, though I'm not sure she got the joke. "I might as well swim some myself," he said, and deposited his fishing gear and clothing on the bank. He waded in deeper. "Damn, it's cold. It's not gonna like being taken under."

That I didn't think a good idea to translate, though the Neanderthal girls might think it was funny. I didn't have the best read on their sense of humor. They did watch 'it' go under, maybe a little too attentively, and I think there was even a soft snicker from Hill Goat when he shivered.

Felipe was, as it is usually put, well-endowed. Yeah, of course I noticed. Whether that made any real difference to any of these women was doubtful but Kat claimed they did call him 'Big Worm' for a while. The name didn't seem to stick and for that we should all be grateful.

Once he was submerged it was out of sight, out of mind. Kat doffed her clothes too and jumped in. "I watch," proclaimed Hill Goat. It was probably just as well someone stood guard.

\* \* \*

We approached the cliffs toward mid-afternoon. Not a single fish to show for our trip but that didn't matter. Purely on a whim I had dug around and found a few mussels. Pearl mussels, I think they were, but I'm not knowledgeable of European species. They'd become somewhat scarce in my time, the future. Endangered. Not a problem sixty thousand years ago. We'd wrapped them up to take home. I knew they weren't good to eat—not poisonous but nasty tasting. Our Neanderthals knew that too. But the shells could be useful for tools. Or jewelry. I think that's what Hill Goat had in mind for them.

"So who's climbing up there?" I asked. "Not you, Rabbit. One brush with death today is enough for you."

I was surprised when Felipe began to scramble up the escarpment. Agile for an old guy. Well, older than me. Doves scattered in alarm. He came to a ledge and turned around to sit on it, facing us. "Nicu-da'a!" exclaimed Rabbit. Kat and Hill Goat both burst into laughter.

"Huh?" was my response.

"Nicu-da'a," repeated Kat. "Condor. Felipe looks like a big bald-headed condor perched up there."

So he did. "You have a new name," I called up to him. "You're Condor from now on."

"An improvement. The egg has hatched!" He looked beside him. "No eggs here but a nest full of squabs. Fat little fellows." Without ceremony, he stuffed them in his bag and went looking for more.

He raided three nests before we headed home.

# 13.

A FOX PELT WAS DRYING before the cave mouth. We were accustomed to seeing skins there, on stretchers made of string and willow wand. Rabbits or pretty much any small furred animal would be skinned. The Neanderthals wasted nothing.

"We baited a snare with part of a rabbit we'd already caught," explained Bob-Raven. "The old fox never saw that coming."

"I suppose old fox is on the menu tonight," commented Kat.

"Let's hope it's actually young and tender," I added to that.

The man grimaced. "I'll leave that to you two. What was that Egg was carrying in?"

"Plump squabs. I'd bet they're way more appetizing than fox. Oh, and his name now is Condor."

I had an idea Rabbit had already informed half the cave of this fact. That didn't mean the moniker would stick.

The chamois skin was also drying. What had become of the skull and horns? The latter might be useful for some sort of toolmaking, maybe. I didn't know. The meat had all been consumed, of course, right down to cracking the bones for their marrow, not to mention various internal organs.

Hmm, that had included the brains. Probably the skull had been bashed open with a hand ax. It wouldn't be hanging on the wall as a trophy.

Someone quacked. I looked around to see Acorn with a mischievous grin on her face. "Quack! Quack!" Or the Neanderthal equivalent. She turned and scampered off. I was mystified.

Kat and Hill Goat had a murmured conference. They seemed just as baffled. A further conference followed with little Nut Grass who sat grinning at us. He might have wanted to quack too.

"Ah." Kat nodded her head in understanding. "Rabbit informed anyone who would listen that you swam like a duck. I think Duck is a much nicer name than Lynx."

"If you call me that I will sue your employers," I threatened. "I'm sure that wasn't covered in the contract." Then my mind moved sideways. "Hey, are there ducks around? We could try hunting them."

Another exchange between the two women. "Mostly in the fall and spring, the same as the reindeer. The tribe calls them the seasons of the reindeer." Hill Goat added some more and Kat nodded. "Some of both come through here but far more by what she calls the great stream. I suspect that would be the proto-Tiber."

I had my doubts this tribe of women and children would journey that far. And I realized I would never know. "You have seen the great stream?" I asked Hill Goat. As best I could.

More fast-paced language that I couldn't begin to follow. Kat translated. "Two years ago. Fall?" She and the young woman exchanged some more words. "No, it was spring. The whole tribe went. The men went back in the fall by themselves, for there had been trouble with others who lived there. And—" She listened a moment. "Um, the next time the men went away they did not come back."

Spring of last year, I assumed. Slain by another tribe? These people had shown little tendency toward violence. I hadn't seen anyone hit anyone, despite Dusk Light's threats against Yukey. Nor even heard much harsh language, for that matter. But when it came to defending scarce resources, things might change.

Or they could have had a run-in with a herd of mammoths or any of a dozen other scenarios. Disease could even have played a role.

They were gone. We were here. That was what mattered now. We went on into the cave.

* * *

Ice Age life filled the next couple days. An idyllic life? So it seemed to us though we knew it could be brutally hard as well. We hunted and gathered, learned and taught, played in both the day and night. Out hosts felt confident to forage further afield for the fruits and seeds of the season.

The folk of the tribe had already noticeably filled out in the week we had been with them. The weight they were putting on now might make the difference between survival and death in the harsh winter months to come. But I wanted to leave them more. We needed to hunt again, one more 'real' hunt before we left. Maybe we could bag something large. If not, several things not so large.

First though, there was Dog Wolf's initiation. Yukey and Felipe did not take great interest in the ceremony but Bob became enthusiastically involved. Maybe he still wanted to be the tribal shaman.

"This ritual is as much for us as the boy," I told them. "Another Neanderthal experience."

Bob smiled at that. "Even if we are making it up."

"We'll have to depend on you for that. Making things up is your trade."

He nodded slowly. Thoughtfully, even. "I have some ideas. It's completely dark down in that hole, huh? We'll have to do something with light. Hmm. Yeah."

One thing to be said for him is that he understood symbolism. Naturally, we also depended on the knowledge of Kat and Jad.

Such as it was. Jad had remained completely hands-off on the initiation so far, other than promising to take part. Bob and I went to speak with them. "There doesn't seem to be a tribal totem," said Jad. "Whether the men had individual totem animals, I don't know."

"Didn't Dog Wolf say something about the Great Bear?" I asked.

"That's more along the lines of a god. The closest thing these folk have to one."

Kat nodded. "Great Bear seems to have been known in many places, as well as to the moderns who moved in later. Whether they learned of him from the Neanderthals or came up with him on their own is impossible to tell."

"Maybe they should have a god," spoke Bob. "Something obvious, like the sun." Incidentally, some were calling him Fox Catcher now. Fox Catcher Raven.

We told Dog Wolf nothing of any of this. We did let the women know what we intended.

* * *

It was the night of our tenth day. No, more properly, the morning of our eleventh, hours before the dawn. We had nabbed a sleeping Dog Wolf and carried him outside without speaking.

He spoke for a little while but settled down on receiving no answers. The boy had never gone far from the cave when it was dark. Fear and curiosity both were close to bubbling over but he remained subdued, trekking northward with us.

It was dangerous, to be sure, to go wandering out into the night. I wasn't particularly concerned about those we left in the cave. They could take care of themselves and had been fore-warned.

And if one of us died? Or all of us, for that matter? No matter. We'd just pop back to our own time. All but the Wolf Dog. He was the only one who could really be killed. If he did go on after we left. That remained uncertain.

If any creature watched our little torch-lit procession pass by, it did not make itself known. I heard nothing but owls, distant, down near the stream.

"Here it is," whispered Felipe Condor. It was the first any of us had spoken since leaving the cave. We couldn't keep our silence forever, even if it might have made the whole thing more effec-tive. I hoped nothing had taken up residence since last we were here. Rousing a bear in the darkness would not help our cere-mony go smoothly.

We had worked up a ceremony. Mostly Bob had worked it up and we added some ideas. Each knew what we were to do. We had to depend on Jad, he who best knew the dialect, to speak for us.

But Felipe and I had to actually lead, having already explored the place some. I went first. It had been my idea, after all. "The bats are out still. I'd like to come up here in the evening and see them emerge." Although it would be just as dangerous to be hanging out here as night fell.

"I would assume they hibernate in here through the winter," said Jad, climbing down behind me, using a knotted rope of mixed animal and plant fiber. He surveyed the chamber. "There will be exploration of this cave when we return. No one knows of it."

"I still haven't explored past the next chamber. There might be much more beyond it." I thought maybe to come back before we returned to the future. No, that wouldn't be necessary and there were better uses of my time. "Ha, I can wait until we get back to go further. I would not mind at all being involved in its exploration." It was one thing to look forward to, in that world.

"But there will be no trace of us ever visiting it." I knew that. We all did. The six of us stood in the small initial cave. It was time to begin.

We led Dog Wolf into the next cave. He was properly awed by the place, glittering in the light of our torches. "Sit," order Jad.

The boy searched our faces a moment for a clue of what might be to come. We remained impassive though I, at least, had to keep myself from snickering. "Here you will be buried in the earth, the mother of us all, and then reborn as a man," proclaimed Jad. "Let darkness be!"

With that we silently filed out, leaving the lad alone. To his credit, he stayed put and made no complaint. I'm not sure I would have but I've always tended toward being contrary. Up the rope and into the open air, the black star-filled sky arched above. I had never seen stars so clearly until we came here, sixty thousand years in the past, before the lights of cities veiled our skies.

"Get away from the entry," said Bob Fox Catcher Raven. "We don't want any light finding its way in."

We walked to a spot a few yards away. "How long, do you reckon?" asked Yukey.

"Till we see some sign of dawn. We'll bring him out at sunrise."

"About an hour, I'd say," Jad added. "We might as well sit down and wait. And douse some of your torches. One or two are enough."

We could have done this in the daytime, it is true. It was pitch black in that second room any time. The symbolism of the rising sun had appealed to Bob and me. Maybe an adventure into the night had too.

I needed to relieve myself and stepped a little distance away from the others. Was their some sort of tremor beneath my feet? A faint vibration. And now sounds, coming from the darkness, of breathing, of heavy feet meeting the ground.

Something large loomed up before me, something covered in

shaggy reddish hair. The torch light reflected from its huge curving tusks. It stopped to peer at me with little glittering eyes before raising its trunk and trumpeting.

A mammoth!

# 14.

THE GREAT BEAST WHEELED and disappeared into the night.

"I wonder if that sound made it down to Wolf Dog," mused Bob. "It would certainly add to the experience."

I didn't care much about the boy at the moment. I'd just had my own ceremony, my own initiation. The others didn't seem so awed. They hadn't been as close.

Jad looked toward where the creature had vanished. "I've seen only one on previous trips. A young bull. This might be the same mammoth."

There was not yet any sign of dawn.

We waited until a touch of rose appeared above the hill. Birds began greeting it all about us. "Let's finish," I said, and entered the cave mouth. Going down into Dog Wolf's symbolic womb. No torch but Jad's was lit as we gathered below.

Some of the bats had returned. Only the rustling of their wings broke the silence. We filed into the next space behind Jad, and formed a circle around the seated Wolf Dog. He looked up at us, uncertain how to react. Jad lit my torch and I that of Condor, who stood beside me, and on around the ring until all five torches filled the place with their light

"Rise," spoke Jad. "I name you Spear Maker." We had decided on that title for him. The boy was rightfully proud of having created a flint-tipped spear for himself.

Which I now handed to him, having carried it along. "Bear Chaser names you Spear Maker," I intoned.

"Condor names you Spear Maker."

And so on. Raven stepped forward with a little bowl—made from a marmot skull—filled with an ocher clay, mixed with a little fat. It was sort of a brownish gold, closer to what is known as raw sienna. We were not that far from the city that gave it its name.

He drew a circle with it on Spear Maker's chest. "Like the sun, you rise new this morning." It was a pretty long speech in the Neanderthal dialect. Raven had carefully memorized it. I handed a torch to the boy—or man, now—and Jad lit it from his own.

"Lead us to the light, Spear Maker," he said.

He needn't be asked twice. The ceremony might have gotten a little clumsy as we climbed our rope to the open air; otherwise, it went rather nicely. I had imagined all sorts of scenarios where we messed up one part or another of it.

The sun was just coming over the hilltops.

* * *

I wondered what sort of initiation lay in store for Rabbit. I could ask Wolf Chaser—I called her that rather than Hill Goat, most of the time—but it was surely meant to be a secret from the menfolk. Best not to pry.

We had created a secret ritual for Spear Maker to lead when we were gone. Little Nut Grass might undergo it in a couple or three years. Assuming these people were still here, which was what I preferred to do.

Young Spear Maker did not wash his chest for some time but inevitably the sun flaked off.

As he was now a man, a full-fledged male of the tribe, he

109

would be part of any future hunts. We began the planning of one at once, with him involved all the way. He might have become just a trifle disdainful of Raven's snares for a short time, considering them suited to children and woman, but that didn't last.

"What shall we seek?" I asked our council. Not the mammoth, I hoped!

"Horses," voted Raven.

"Deer," said the Fat Bear. "I want to sample Ice Age venison."

I didn't know the animal Spear Maker named. "The aurochs," translated Jad. "The big bison. Maybe a tad larger than we'd wish to tackle."

Maybe so. Nor did we have any idea where they might be found. That I considered fortunate. Spear casting would largely be up to me and young Spear Maker. I'd provided him with an atlatl, and he practiced with it but was far from skillful. Maybe I was too and my kill had been mostly luck. Not that I'd admit it.

I had also remembered that smaller throwers had been used by humans of this period and had made one up for Rabbit to play with, throwing darts little larger than an arrow. I wouldn't trust anyone younger with such a device. Certainly not Nut Grass.

"We should hunt to the north," I told the others. "I'm not forgetting that lion to the south of us."

"But that's where the horses were, too," Raven pointed out. I did not think he was being serious. In theory, six men with spears should be able to handle a lion. It was not a theory I felt like testing.

So it was decided to set out the next morning, all six of those

110

men with spears. Yes, even Condor. "I might as well get the experience too, before we ship out," he said. We all felt the end coming soon. "But I do intend to fish once more."

"I wouldn't mind giving that another go myself," I replied.

Yeah, the end coming. For me, it was a sense of loss, maybe. I wasn't sure just how it effected the others. Maybe Yukey not much at all.

Tomorrow we would set out, hunt and maybe have success or maybe not. Then things would wind down through our last couple days here. I did not want to let my mate—my mate for a little longer—loose from my embrace that night.

* * *

North we went, as swiftly as possible. We wanted to make this a one-day hunt but recognized we could camp overnight, if need be. Building shelters was not too difficult or we might find a safe place among the rocks. The decision had been to follow the stream into the forest, at least at the start.

That seemed the best place to come across Yukey's deer. Those were most likely to be red deer, as common then in Europe as they were tens of thousands of years later. Reindeer herds would still be north of us, grazing perhaps where the Po flowed in our time.

As for any giant elk, I would just as soon avoid them. They might be even more dangerous than the aurochs.

"Tracks," I told the others. "That's what we need to find. Game trails. Just wandering around hoping to blunder into something is unlikely to work."

"That's how I found my third wife," said Yukey.

"Man, she was lying in wait for you," came Felipe's rejoinder.

Ball actually looked a little offended. He might like to think he was in charge of any situation. That no one could take advantage of him. But he chuckled then, making it seem he dismissed it as nothing more than an old friend's joke.

"So what if we do find tracks?" asked Raven. "Follow them or wait for the critter to come by again?"

"I'd be inclined to follow them toward the water. If we find where animals drink, that's the place to lie in wait for them."

I didn't know if that was actually a good idea. It sounded like a good idea but that's no proof. In truth, I had never hunted anything larger than rabbits and squirrels, when I was a kid.

One did not lie in wait for those by the watering hole. We did find paths among the trees when we penetrated into the forest. I squatted and tried to make out what sort of tracks might have been left.

"That looks like a deer," I said, pointing. It wasn't too large and definitely made by a cloven hoof. As likely a guess as any though in honesty it could be a goat or chamois or even an aurochs calf. We followed the trail in the general direction of the stream.

Spear Maker pointed toward the ground and said, "Wolf." Yeah, that was as likely a guess as any, too. Definitely not someone's poodle.

"If there's game, we have to expect predators," said Raven.

"They're not what we're hunting," Felipe said. "I want something good to eat."

I agreed. "Me too. And not just for us."

That was understood. "A wolf pelt would not go unappreciated," said Jad.

We followed our path into open grassland, a green expanse lying before us. The stream had emerged from the trees. "You're not going to see extended deciduous forest in this time and place," Jad told us. "This little patch is fairly rare. We might see more trees further south."

"Like Sicily?" asked Raven. "Kat said we could walk there without getting wet."

"I do think we'll get wet if we try to get to the stream," said Felipe. "That's marshland ahead of us."

Forms could be seen moving in that open space, none near. "I believe that's our mammoth," said Raven, pointing. "Only one." He might have sounded a little disappointed.

A solitary bull, I figured, if they were like elephants. It didn't matter much. Maybe herds of females and youngsters came this far south in the winter. We wouldn't be here to see it.

What I could see at the moment was a herd of horses. "No chance of sneaking up on those horses," I said.

I understood enough of what Spear Maker said then to get the gist of it. Drive them toward some of us, waiting in ambush. With the tall grass, it might be possible. Marshy ground could be to our advantage too. "We should find a spot where animals cross the water. Position ourselves there."

It didn't take long to find just such a place, a muddy ford. The path we had been following led right to it. "Bob and me," said Jad. "We'll try to circle around them and drive them back here." The rest of us hid among the reeds.

"I have doubts they can get them to run this way," said Yukey. He and I had positioned ourselves on one side, Condor and Spear Maker on the other.

It was a pretty long distance to keep them running the desired direction. Maybe more of us should be driving them. Damn, there were a lot of mosquitoes! Now I could hear the pair crying out, attempting to spook the herd. Not much was visible from here.

Ah, the sound of hooves. They had succeeded in stampeding them, at least. I wouldn't have been too surprised if a recalcitrant stallion had turned the tables and chased the men. Raven and Jad continued to cry out. It was doubtful they could keep up with the animals.

"They're veering away." Yukey did have the sense to whisper. Having hunted deer would have taught him that. I raised myself just a little—I was nearly a head shorter, after all—and tried to spy what was going on. Yes, the horses were running toward the forest, not the stream, despite the men trying to turn them.

"No horse meat tonight," I said. Then came a crashing sound. A moment later, a great elk emerged from the grass, leaping in our direction. Horses were not all that had been spooked.

# 15.

SPEAR MAKER GOT IN the first throw. He rose up and yelled lustily as he let fly, his atlatl snapping forward. It was not a good throw but he did manage to hit the fleeing creature. My spear followed and struck more solidly. The elk's knees buckled. Yukey and Felipe both rushed in to jab. This had been the plan.

I followed but there wasn't much to do. Spear Maker's lance had come loose when the elk fell and he now had it again in his hands, thrusting it between the ribs. My god, the beast was large! Those hooves were surely dangerous. Fortunately, the antlers were still somewhat small and in velvet in this season. It lay still by the time Jad and Raven arrived.

Spear Maker's grin may have been the widest I have ever seen on any face. He was enjoying being a man no end.

"Good work," said Jad, in an even, matter of fact voice. "And not even noon yet."

"No problem getting home before dark." Felipe regarded the carcass for a few moments. "That's a lot to carry home though. We'll have to cut it up, right?"

"At least remove some of the guts," I said. "I wonder what it weighs?"

"About a half-ton," Jad informed me. "Going by the size. They get bigger than this." He chuckled. "According to the literature. I've never dealt with one before."

"Well, let's make it lighter," said Yukey. "I guess we can't hang it up to gut it like a whitetail!"

We got to work with hand axes and flint flakes. Even dressed out, there would still be at least a hundred pounds load for each of us, wouldn't there? "Maybe we could make up some sort of travois to get it back," I said.

Jad and Spear Maker discussed the situation for a minute or more. I couldn't follow them. Not enough words I knew. Jad nodded at last. Well, he didn't nod. This tribe didn't sign assent that way.

"Our young hunter says we should bury most of the kill and carry only what we can easily. More of the tribe can come back to finish butchering it tomorrow."

"A bear could get at it," Felipe pointed out. "Or even wolves."

"Not if we cover it with rocks."

It didn't seem the greatest plan but no one had a better. We had to drag the dead elk—a little lighter now with some of the entrails removed—to firmer ground. That was a good distance, and digging would take time. So would dismembering the carcass. We might not get back to the cave before night after all.

"Hey, we're being followed," said Raven.

Wolves. I could see three. No, there was a fourth over there. They investigated us from a distance but seemed to decide we were too many. The gray forms circled back to the offal we had left behind.

Might they return when they had dealt with that? The smell of blood was certainly an enticement. They might grow bolder come night. We found a solid, rocky spot and hacked up the elk as best we might, taking care not to damage the hide. Could we skin it out entire?

No, none had the skill. Not even Spear Maker. Some of the women would have to return with us tomorrow. At least we wouldn't be required to attempt digging. There were plenty enough loose rocks to heap up, though we had to range a way to find enough and carry them back. It was a pretty big elk. We had pushed it up against an outcropping so rocks needn't be piled all around, and removing the legs meant nothing stuck out. We would take off with what meat we could carry. The haunches, mostly, and some of the organs.

Ah, that would most surely bring the wolves on our trail. Naught to be done about it. Before we covered the elk over entirely, Spear Maker took a hand ax to its skull and got the brains. They seemed tiny compared to the size of the beast from which they came. We shared them there before beginning the hike home.

Prion disease? I wasn't inclined to think about it and it was unlikely in a giant elk of the Pleistocene. The big boy looked healthy anyway.

"Do you think that's enough rocks?" asked Felipe. It had been hard work. We were all exhausted.

"Nothing's going to get through that," said Jad. I wasn't completely sure. A large bear, maybe. There was no sense worrying about it. It was mid-afternoon already.

"Then let's head home," I said. We shouldered our loads and walked south.

* * *

We weren't even halfway back when the wolves showed again.

I was surprised it took that long. The same bunch we'd seen before? There had been five of those, as far as I could tell. A family unit perhaps.

I did not see more than that number now. That proved nothing. The pack wouldn't attack us, not while we were together, no matter how much meat we were carrying on our shoulders. But if one of us got careless and straggled—well, there was no telling.

We were even with the old fishing hole now, emerging from the woods. I felt safer being more in the open. Three or four miles to the cave? That could take two hours laden as we were. Midsummer was nearing and there was a long twilight, but we still might not get there before the dark.

"Keep close," Jad called out.

I could hear Yukey huffing. It was to be expected he would have the least endurance, if only because he carried the most mass. He was also the oldest of us but that doesn't always matter so much. He had gotten into better shape before this foray to the past and the time spent here certainly hadn't hurt his condition; still, he was having trouble keeping up. I saw a gray shadow appear not far behind him as he labored.

"Get up here with us, man!" I growled at him.

"Damn," he swore under his breath. "I carried loads of concrete blocks up six stories when I was a kid. I can haul a bit of meat home!"

"If you can't, drop it. Better to let the wolves have it than eat you."

He only gritted his teeth—quite literally—and marched on. I hadn't been sure Yukey had it in him.

Felipe Condor leaned in and whispered to me, "There was no way Ball was going to lose face in front of us all. His ego's keeping him going."

The wolves weren't stupid. When we bunched up again they melted into the deep grass and heather. We trudged along. An hour yet, in deepening twilight.

A shaggy gray wolf darted toward the rear of our group. One only. As we turned, the rest of the pack charged Spear Maker, in the lead. That sort of thing might have worked better with horses or deer. They might have expected him to bolt.

Four they were. Encumbered with his burden of venison, the boy couldn't get his spear into play at once. Raven reacted first, or maybe he was just closest. He dropped the bag full of organ meats he carried and jabbed at the closest wolf. It yipped, perhaps as much in surprise as pain.

Spear Maker had been knocked to the ground but not bitten. The same can't be said for the meat he'd had across his shoulders! The wolves at once went for that. A pair began to drag it away. Raven was the only one unencumbered enough to go after them.

"Let them go!" called Jad.

"It's not worth it," I added.

He turned back, slowly, obviously reluctant. He knew we were right. No more wolves appeared along our way home. And the women in the cave did not need to know we had lost some of our meat.

"We shall go at dawn for the rest," announced Spruce Tree. I hoped it was still there.

We got the dried blood off us as well as we could with sand and grass. I'm sure we all stank of it but I wasn't going to go out for a midnight swim.

\* \* \*

We did indeed go at dawn for the rest of the meat. Everyone, right down to She Bear's infant. You would have thought we were going to a party.

Needless to say, the children slowed us down a little. I didn't mind. It was the last time I would see this land. I really should revisit it when we returned to our time. I would like to walk through modern Umbria, to see what had changed, what was the same.

"I do intend to come back tomorrow morning and fish again," said Felipe Condor as we peered down at our pool. We were progressing along the slopes, well above it. "And then—we say goodbye, don't we?"

I could do no more than slowly nod. I didn't have words to express how I felt about it.

"For me," he went on, "this is not so different from some other vacations I have had, fishing trips. Enjoyable but I know they have an end. I think it has become more than that to you."

"It has. I won't deny that." I wondered how Bob felt. He had bonded some here too. Ah, but he would make sense of it all by writing about it, and move on.

At that moment I wished I had never chosen to come.

Our cache proved unmolested. It was not quite mid-morning when we began to remove the piled rocks. The Neanderthal women, to the surprise of none of us, proved adroit at skinning out the great elk. Or deer, I believe the scientist types call it now. The Giant Deer. That doesn't have the same ring, does it? The venison would taste the same, even if we called it an Irish Elk.

It was indeed a party for them and for the children. There was laughter and joking. Oh, yes, these people joked. They did not lack a sense of humor. There was tuneless singing. There was a certain amount of eating. I had difficulty feeling festive myself.

So, soon after noon, we were on our way back. My own load today was relatively light; I wanted to keep the spear ready. Not that I expected wolves this day but I recognized they could be out there. Bears, too. I worried if any child got more than a few feet away from our column and admonished them.

The heaviest load was that of the hide. That took two to carry, hung across a branch supported on their shoulders. Turns were taken for this. No one grumbled about bearing the load for a time, nor any load. Again, they chattered and sang.

Very little had been left behind. Every part of this great animal could be useful. "This will go a long way toward getting them through the harder times to come," Kat told me. "An animal this size can be turned into quite a lot of jerky."

But not enough to get them through the winter. They would need to continue hunting. A lot would be on the shoulders of young Spear Maker.

The going back was slower but we reached home well before

darkness fell. The entry had been entirely closed up behind us to prevent curious bears or other pests from investigating the cave. Rocks and brush were now removed and the processing of the meat and hide and bones began at once. I chose to go down to the stream and clean myself.

I was not the only one. Others came and went. The Neanderthals did wash in this weather, as I've mentioned before, including their hair. What did they do to remain clean in winter? They might be a pretty stinky bunch come spring.

I wouldn't know. I keep saying that, don't I?

# 16.

RABBIT HAD LEARNED TO make, set and tend the snares. She dragged a marmot into the cave and deposited it proudly before us.

Then she eyed Condor's fishing pole. He had it finished about as well as was possible now. "Go fishing with you?" she asked.

There was no reason not to let her come. Or anyone else who wished. My Wolf Chaser declined. There was work to be done.

My Wolf Chaser. Not mine much longer. I would have liked to spend this day in her company. I *would* have tonight and a bit of tomorrow morning. Then we would no longer exist here. Or here would no longer exist. It came to the same thing.

Our only other companion turned out to be Rabbit's big brother. Spear Maker might have been intrigued by her report of me swimming like a duck. Jad and Kat were far more interested is watching the women process the elk. I have no doubt it was meticulously recorded.

I savored what I could. If the morning were a little too cool, if there were a misty rain coming out of the north, so be it. All that, too, was a part of being in this world.

"You have no one to return to, do you, Ken?" asked Felipe.

I shook my head. No wife. No kids. Not even a business to distract me anymore. "How about you?"

"A wife. A mistress. A daughter in college. Many who call themselves my friends." From his tone I suspected he did not always reciprocate. "My life is satisfying enough."

"Oh? And how does your wife feel about your mistress?"

"We have been married, happily enough, for more than twenty years. And I have always been faithful to both my wife and my mistress." That sounded like both a joke and the truth.

"Loyalty is good," was my only remark.

"It is important to me."

That, too, sounded like the truth. "Ball has a wife, right? His third? It doesn't, ah, sound like loyalty is quite so important to him."

"Only loyalty to himself. He discards anyone no longer useful." He gave me a wry smile. "I guess he thinks I'm still useful. Yukey does have some kids. A lot like him but without his veneer of charisma."

"I'm glad I haven't met them." We went on a little further in silence. Our silence; Rabbit and her brother were chattering on about something.

"Bob has no one waiting either," I said.

"His books are his children. I know artists like Bob."

"Yeah." Maybe I should try to write a book. I could see holing up in my cabin, the only remnant of my former life, and attempting it. "I wonder if that old pike is waiting for me down there."

We descended the slope toward the pond

* * *

The tribe feasted that night. Much meat was consumed.

If we travelers did not eat so much it was because we knew food awaited us in another world. Tomorrow. It was best to leave as much for these people as we could. I attempted to put aside my sense of impending loss and celebrate with them. I could sing too, if I wished. I had learned it was permissible for males, so why not? Never mind that I have no voice to speak of and pretty much only knew country songs. *You Are My Sunshine* went over okay in the Paleolithic.

Last Star sat down beside Bob Raven. What a time for it to happen! I thought for a moment he might rise and move away from her. Maybe it would be better if there was no bond to be broken in a few hours.

But he stayed put. All these women had a bond with us. Not just sexual. Far from it. We had, as Jad had promised when first we came together, become one tribe. They were real people to me. They felt more real than those who lived sixty millennia later.

I would have to describe them in that book I had decided to write. I hoped the memories lasted. I hoped they remained this real.

* * *

"We must—go away for a time," I said to Spear Maker. How else could I put it? I wasn't going to say we would never return, even though it was true.

Jad translated this for me and then told the boy, "You must take care of the tribe while we are gone." Had he come to believe they continued when we left? The man had seemed skeptical of the idea.

Maybe, as I, he but hoped they lived on.

I had attempted to say something of the same sort to Wolf Chaser Hill Goat last night. There was no way to make her understand what I didn't understand myself. I could only make love. I could only hold her tight one last time.

As a group, we had left the cave, giving no hint we would not return. Spear Maker had accompanied us down to the water. There we made our farewell to him. He watched us cross the stream before turning back to the cave. To his people.

Over the low hill beyond we climbed, heading back to the spot where we arrived. This was not necessary. Jad felt it best we disappear in the direction from which we came, but any place concealed from the tribe's eyes would have done. Even that probably didn't matter. He held up a hand to signal a stop. "This is far enough." We stood knee-deep in the heather and waited.

"As required," announced our guide, "I shall again call our roll for the official record." Jad went through the list of our names as he had before. "And Jadunath Palit," he finished. "Here, once again." He looked at his watch. "Soon. About ten minutes."

None of us had any words. My head was too full of thoughts for them. We waited, waited on a beautiful Ice Age morning in an unspoiled world. The same crows that had greeted us now seemed to caw a farewell.

"Here we go," Jad almost whispered. The world around us misted, as it had when we came. I could just begin to glimpse the room in the facility, back in our time, the room from which we had departed. There were shadowy human figures.

Then all came into focus again. That cold machine-filled room of the future disappeared and we still stood in a field in Paleolithic Italy.

Again, none of us had any words.

# PART II.
# THE PRIZES OF
# PRIMEVAL HUNTS

## 17.

BOB SAT DOWN. THERE was a slight, knowing smile on his face.

Anger began to appear on Euclid Ball's visage. "What the hell happened? If we're delayed getting back there's going to be hell to pay!"

"Did something go wrong?" Kat asked. "Was the return time set wrong?"

Palit shook his head. "I've never heard of this happening. Wait. We're bound to pop back."

Bob Raven gave him a sort of sidelong look. "We already did," he said. "You saw it."

"But we came back?"

"No. We made it home and stayed there. We also stayed here—an alternate version of ourselves in a new time line. That's my guess, anyway."

He might have been thinking of this possibility already, I realized. He might even have expected or at least hoped it would happen.

"So we would be in both places at once," I said. "Sort of. Hmm, and our other selves would never know."

I don't think Yukey got it. He seemed all baffled rage.

And Jad didn't seem to want to believe it. "Let's give it some more time," he said. We all sat down with Bob and waited. With Raven. If we were indeed here to stay—and I was beginning to believe he was right—we might as well forget those names from another life and another time.

I was okay with the idea. If that other version of me, the one that went home, knew what I was up to he would be envious. I think I got the better part of it when our ways split. The road less traveled.

He—I?—might soon be sitting in my cabin, reminiscing about his two weeks as a Neanderthal. Wondering if Hill Goat still existed and what she might have done after he left.

And in that world where he existed there would have been another Hill Goat who never met me. A Hill Goat who disappeared with all her tribe sixty thousand years earlier. There would be at least one Hill Goat for each group of time travelers who had visited the tribe before. Ha, each of those groups of tourists would also have been stranded in new time lines their presence had created, wouldn't they? There might be hundreds, thousands, of differing time lines, each with its own Hill Goat.

They might even be infinite. That was too much to grasp and unimportant, ultimately. I was here and it seemed I would remain.

We kicked the idea Raven had presented back and forth, our

voices low, almost hushed. "So there could be another me that went home," said Yukey, at last. "Hard to believe but I get it. And everyone will think it's me."

"It is you," Raven reminded him.

"Yeah." The big man got up and brushed himself off. "I hope he sues your company good, Palit," he said, and laughed uproariously.

Jad rose too. "We might as well go back. Maybe Bob's right and maybe he isn't, but there's no sense in sitting on a hillside."

"We're all Neanderthals from now on," Kat stated.

Condor spoke up. "But we needn't be. We could strike out any direction we wished and be on our own. We could go visit those modern men you say are across the sea."

"That's a pretty long walk to the tip of Sicily. And then we'd have to build a raft or something to get us over to Africa."

"We may not have the survival skills for it, either," added Raven. "I'm for staying with our tribe."

I agreed to this. "If we travel, better to travel with them."

So it was, on an early afternoon in summer, a sunny afternoon in another time, a time far beyond human memory, we returned to our tribe.

* * *

Spear Maker was disappointed. We hadn't even been gone overnight. "We'll never leave again," Raven promised him.

"Or if we do, you'll come along," I added to this. All still being translated, for the most part, by Jad and Kat. That would have to change. We truly must learn the language of our tribe now.

131

We also must learn just where we stand in the tribe. Raven and I had mates. That helped with our own integration. Would the others choose to settle down with women? And what of Kat, for that matter?

Fat Bear had apparently been thinking along the same lines. "Who is going to be in charge here?" he asked. "Jad? His authority no longer applies if we're not going back."

"Spruce Tree," answered Raven. "For now."

"I agree," I said. Condor nodded as well.

"That makes sense," said Kat. Jad only shrugged. I don't think he was quite ready to abdicate, nor even admit things had changed.

"We could always vote on our own choices," Raven offered.

"Any one of us can vote by walking away," Condor stated. "No one is going to be bound by any decisions."

"Only those that are good for the entire tribe," I said. "From here out I think we need to confer more with the women. We can't just decide what to do when it pleases us."

Kat approved. "It's a matter of our survival as well as theirs. We're tied together now."

I considered her for a moment. "Maybe we should think of you a tribal matron from now on, too."

"She needs the proper cicatrix," Raven observed.

"What's that?" growled the Bear.

"The scar the women all have on their left arm. It's a part of their coming of age ritual, I would hazard."

That scar consisted of a sort of wavy line, a little snake of scar tissue. "Maybe we should introduce real tattooing to them," said Condor. "I have a few, as you've noticed." More than a few.

"Or I could just paint one on," said Kat. "I suppose I need an actual Neanderthal name too. No one has seen fit to bestow one on me."

"What is cat in their language?" asked Raven. "I know there are little wild cats around."

Kat didn't seem to like that one. "They'll find some reason to call you something, sometime," said Jad. "If only Crow. Me too."

As it turned out, someone heard Kat whistling a couple days later, down by the stream, and dubbed her Blackbird. The name took. Blackbirds were common here in the summer.

Kat was smaller than the adult women of the tribe. Not shorter, but more lightly built. She was also darker, as were Jad and Condor. Condor had those tattoos up and down his arms—nowhere else—but these had brought no comment. Which is not to say the kids didn't stare at them sometimes.

We sat down that first night after our 'return' to eat with the others. "You're going to keep posing as a couple?" Condor asked Jad and Kat.

"For now," was the answer from Kat. The two sat together, as before. I did not know if that would continue or whether they had partners in their previous lives. Future lives? Whatever.

Condor seemed to consider this for a moment or two. Then he gave them a brusque nod and without the least hesitation went to sit down beside Dusk Light. He'd made up his mind to deal with our changed situation. The woman did not rebuff him.

That meant only Fat Bear had made no choice. Or Spruce Tree and She Bear had made no choices. Someone would eventually, I assumed.

We were still working on the more perishable parts of the elk. Any meat that could be dried was undergoing that process. There remained some organ meats, some bony parts that weren't worth scraping for the bits of flesh that clung to them. Bones were being split for marrow. Carefully, for some could be useful for tools. It was too bad the antlers were not mature enough.

And this was my life now. Yesterday I had wished for it, not believing it possible. It was daydream, an idle yearning for the unattainable. As the cave fell into darkness, the fire reduced to embers, most retiring to their beds, Jad came and sat beside me. Wolf Chaser had already left my side to take first turn at sentry duty.

"We must hold a council tomorrow to decide how we are to proceed," he said. "If we are indeed stuck here, we'll need to have places and roles among these people. I think there is no question that you should lead our hunting."

That did seem sensible. "And there is plenty of hunting to be done," I responded. Nothing more. Things would sort themselves out. If we were to survive, they would have to.

Jad sat silently for a minute before saying, "I was going to suggest, when we had returned to the future, that you might consider training for my job. You would be good at it." He shrugged. "Maybe I did suggest it."

And maybe I accepted. But I knew that other Ken Sasaki would never return to this setting, having once lost it. I rose and went to my Wolf Chaser.

* * *

"I should learn flint working too," claimed Raven. "Maybe we all should."

"No doubt. Until we have a source of flint there won't be much opportunity," Jad told him.

We sat, we travelers, beside the stream. A few of the Neanderthals were near but we spoke in English so they had no idea what was going on. "There are all sorts of resources we need to locate," I reminded them. I turned to Kat. "Aren't there other sorts of stones that can be used?"

"Chert and Chalcedony. Obsidian, of course," she said. "Some others. Basalt? Maybe."

"Chalcedony? Isn't that used in jewelry or something?" asked Condor.

"It's like opal," said Fat Bear, and looked toward Kat. "Right? My first wife had some trinkets made of it."

"Sort of the same thing. Just as flint is basically a form of chert. I know flint quarries existed over near the Adriatic coast."

"There is chert in Tuscany," Jad said. He shrugged and smiled. "There may be some in the next valley over for all we know. It may be embedded in the rock beneath our feet."

"This tribe certainly has nothing to trade for any, if that's how they got it before," I said.

"Some decent furs might do the trick," felt Raven.

Kat shook her head. "We don't even know if there was trade

between tribes. Flint and tools did travel from place to place but they could have been carried on migrations, or even stolen."

"Very well," spoke Jad. "We'll certainly keep an eye out for some sort of stone for tools. And we're agreed to put Ken, I mean Lynx, in charge of hunting."

I corrected him. "Of organizing hunting parties. We're all free to hunt on our own when we feel like it." In as amiable a voice as I could muster, I added, "Just as we are free to go our own ways even if we acknowledge you as our leader."

"Our leader but not our boss," said Condor.

Jad might have been trying to rival me in amiability. "I recognize I have no authority over any of you. Nor should I. We would do better to follow the lead of our tribal matrons."

"For now," agreed Fat Bear. The words were spoken lightly but I sensed the seriousness behind them.

So we split. Our real Stone Age Life perhaps began that moment, when we all agreed to live with this tribe, to work with this tribe. Now it was time to learn how to live that life fully. Time to learn the language we would speak the rest of our lives, most likely. Time to learn the ways of life when man was young.

Raven and the Bear wandered off toward the cave. They seemed more friendly than I had noted before.

Condor looked at their receding figures for a moment. "Ball needs to be on top in any situation. That's just his nature. He'll charm and bully his way to what he wants." He turned back to us. "Watch out for him."

"We will have to watch out for many things in this world," I said.

# 18.

WE DIDN'T HUNT RIGHT away. Not in the sense of an all-hands-on-deck hunting party. I chose to scout out the area over the next few days, watching for game but more interested in learning the lay of the land. Jad usually came with me. Sometimes Spear Maker. He was as likely to be with Raven, who spent much time with the older children, chasing small game, checking the snares, making their own explorations. It was a different way of learning the life but perhaps one just as valid.

That we were consuming more than we brought in was obvious. I couldn't expect to bring another elk to the tribe but there should be plenty more game. We should be able to harvest some reindeer when fall came. Maybe we could even get over to the 'great stream,' the proto-Tiber, to take some. That would be a considerable journey—my guess would be about thirty miles over the hills—and probably one the tribe should take as a whole.

And do so before it grew too cold. These Neanderthals, I knew, could withstand the winter weather better than we who came from another world. We were less likely to survive in this harsh environment.

I wondered if salmon of some sort came up the river. Not this far but below the pond. Or any other fish. Eels, maybe? What if we could travel on to the sea? There would be clams there, I was sure. We had the shells to prove it. What sort of fish swam the Mediterranean sixty thousand years ago I couldn't guess. I didn't even know what swam it in my own time.

That sea lay at least twice as far beyond the great river as the river did from our cave. A hundred miles, all total, perhaps. That would not do for this year. We must attend to our immediate needs.

One of those was language. We all made the attempt to learn the dialect of our adopted tribe. Some more successfully than others, to be sure. A pidgin of sorts was developing, our English and their language, especially among the youngsters. It would surely grow into a new tongue, spoken by generations to come. And then? Disappear as it mixed back into the dialects around it, no doubt.

Be that as it might, we were becoming able to communicate more clearly. I'll admit I was not one of the quickest learners. Fat Bear, on the other hand, proved quite adept and was soon charming all the women of the tribe. All but Dusk Light. She made no attempt to hide her dislike of the man.

He seemed to 'work' on Spruce Tree, in particular. She and She Bear remained without mates and I noted the Bear chose not to be intimate with either. Not yet. That would surely not continue. And what of the situation with Jad and Kat?

I held off bringing that up with Kat for a couple days but, eventually, in a private moment down by the stream, I asked, "Does Jad have a wife back, um, did he have a wife?"

"A husband. Our Jad is gay. He had sex with Spruce Tree purely as a duty." She gave me a wry smile. "I can understand why she might not have been overwhelmed by his lovemaking."

"Oh."

Before I could come up with further comment, she said, "And

don't tell anyone else. I'm telling you this so you can make informed decisions."

I nodded. Kat put more trust in me than I was inclined to put in myself. "Did you have someone? Or shouldn't I ask?"

There was silence. Kat sat and looked at the rapidly flowing water. For a moment, I thought maybe she would say nothing. "There was a boyfriend. I don't know that I miss him that much. Maybe I'll hook up with one of you guys down the line." Again with the smile. "Or wait for Spear Maker to grow up a little more."

"I believe he's looking forward to that. There's not going to be anyone else around for him. The only girl nearing maturity is his sister."

"Unless we meet up with another tribe. It seems common for individuals to move from one to another for a mate. That's why you boys showing up didn't perturb our women too much And—" Another moment of hesitation. "Polygamy seems to be tolerated, after a fashion. I need to speak more with the women about it but it does seem sharing is expected when the numbers are uneven. For both sexes."

I was not surprised. "I don't think any of that matters too much right now, when we are all going to be kept busy. Things may sort themselves out when we hole up in the winter."

"That they may."

* * *

The whole tribe came out to gather berries. This Jad had suggested, though I had suggested it to him. I did not intend to assert any authority save when it came to hunting. Balance of power or something like that.

To be sure, the women actually organized things, and it was they and the children who did most of the gathering. We menfolk stood guard. And babysat, keeping an eye out that the littlest ones didn't stray. I had carved more atlatls for our use. None were in any way adept with them, at least not yet. In honesty, Wolf Chaser threw better with one than any of the males, Spear Maker included.

She had taken a large bird with one just yesterday. I had no idea what it might be but Jad identified it as a bustard. The Neanderthals, of course, had their own name for it. It was not particularly tasty.

"We should have gotten back here sooner," Jad confided to me. "These blackberries are definitely past their peak."

That I could see. It wasn't to be helped; after all, we hadn't expected to be here. "There must be other fruit ripening."

"According to the women, there should be quite a lot of bilberries in about a month." He chuckled. "A moon, maybe I should say. I assume they are bilberries from the description."

Bilberries? I knew absolutely nothing about them aside from the name. Jad must have recognized that from my blank expression.

"Similar to blueberries. Small but worth picking anyway."

There were many thickets of brambles but the women sensibly stayed together, moving from one spot to the next. Between them and us, we managed to keep the children contained. My eyes were more often on them than elsewhere. "I've seen grape vines," I said.

He nodded. "So have I. There are all sorts of edibles out there we don't know about. The tribe will be aware of them." He surveyed the open land on the gentle slope above us for a moment. "I think we might find date palms a little further south. Maybe figs too, and wild olives."

"If not, we could still go visit Africa! Hey—" I lowered my voice to a near whisper. "I saw something moving in the trees down that way." I pointed. "I don't think any of our people have gone that far." And they shouldn't have, if they did.

"Our people, is it? I guess that's so." I wasn't sure if Jad was amused by the idea. "Let's take a look."

I hoped it might be a deer or a horse or something else tasty. Or it could be a wolf or other predator. Either way, it should be investigated. We had been working our way down the valley floor, near the stream, where most of the blackberries grew. I had wanted to start at the other end and work back toward our cave but the women would have none of that. I don't think it made any sense to them.

We did think differently at times, it was true. Still, these Neanderthals were far more like us than they were dissimilar, and those differences might be more cultural than intrinsic to who they were. They had learned to think in certain ways and weren't likely to change. They were like most modern humans in that, too.

Most of the trees here, as further upstream, were willows. A few birch stood. We should have another expedition to gather bark, sometime. We skirted another blackberry patch, fairly small, and entered a copse of young head-high willow. They grew thickly.

Grunting? Were there pigs here? I would love some pork! I motioned Jad to move off a little to my left, closer to the stream. I held my spear ready though there would be no room to use the atlatl in this thicket, or cast the spear at all, for that matter.

I pushed a branch aside with my left arm and found myself face to face with a rather large brown bear. He was certainly as surprised as I, for he backed up with a 'woof.' I stopped still, holding the spear out before me.

When I say large, I mean larger than me. Larger by quite a bit! I do not think it rivaled a run of the mill grizzly. For a moment, we eyed each other. Then Jad burst from the thicket to its right. The bear wheeled about and scooted into the brush.

I stood there staring toward where it had disappeared for a few seconds before I realized how quickly my heart was beating. I made myself take a deep, slow breath, and then another.

Jad came to stand beside me. He looked in the direction the bear had run off and then to me. "Are you all right?"

I nodded. I might not have been if he hadn't shown up. A lesson to always hunt in partnership! "That may be the young fellow who poked his nose into the cave," I said, trying to sound calm. "We should keep an eye out for him and maybe try to, um, harvest him come fall. He should be good and fat then." Barbe-cued bear might be as good as barbecued pig.

"I wonder if he remembered you swatting him."

So did I, and whether it would be a good or a bad thing. "Let's get back to the tribe," I said.

* * *

"The Bear faces a dilemma," said Condor. "I am sure he would prefer the younger She Bear but Spruce Tree is the matriarch of the tribe. He might see her as a path to power." He let that sink in for a few seconds before adding, "It would be better if you claimed her, Jad."

Jad's answer came with no trace of emotion. "She might just turn me down. And there is Kat to consider." I knew what underlay that statement but it had been told to me in confidence.

"Hmm. Do you and Kat need to keep up that pretense any longer? Maybe you two should just sit separately from now on."

"It's best they don't," I put in. "We needn't go into the reasons now. And I think we need to name her Blackbird from here out."

Condor accepted this with a shrug. "Plus," he went on, "She Bear is sister to my mate. You can be sure he sees me as a rival. Me and Jad. I don't think he takes you and Raven too seriously."

Jad smiled slightly at that but said nothing. The three of us followed along on the heels of the homeward-returning tribe, their rear guard. Young Nut Grass ambled beside us. He could not be trusted to carry any berries home. They would surely arrive in his stomach.

"And then, Raven is mate to Spruce Tree's daughter. That brings him closer to power, at least in Fat Bear's eyes. He might like to make Raven an ally of sorts."

"He seems to be working on that already," I said. Jad nodded. We'd all seen the Bear being the author's best buddy.

Yipping arose from the higher ground to our left, yipping that turned to howls.

"Wolf," announced Nut Grass. "I'll kill them!" He shook his spear. Or sharpened stick.

"There's lots of daylight left," I said, or attempted to in the tribal dialect. "They shouldn't bother us."

"They might one of these days," said Jad.

"It might be well to hunt them first. We have Nut Grass to help us." I gave the boy a grin.

"Best not to encourage him," Jad told me, in English. "Nut Grass might do something he shouldn't." He turned to the boy. "You need to wait until you're a man."

"Soon!"

# 19.

THE FORMER EUCLID BALL had become healthier-looking and leaner in our time here. Still heavy though—no one seemed willing to name him anything other than Fat Bear.

Fat Bear had taken a seat beside Spruce Tree one night. The woman had seemed hesitant for a moment but then accepted him. The choice slightly surprised me, but Condor had called it. The Bear was attracted to power, even the leadership of a small Stone Age tribe.

That left She Bear without a mate. It didn't seem to perturb her. Yet. And Fat Bear continued to flirt with her and, to some degree, the other women. I doubted he would go further than that for now. He would not chance offending Spruce Tree.

To the rest of us—that is Condor and Jad and me, mostly—the Bear could be surly. He did not want to take direction from anyone and when he did, he did it with ill grace.

We mostly ignored him. Or we pretended to. Condor knew the man best so I sort of looked to him to take the lead on dealing with him. Jad didn't want to lead at all anymore, or so it seemed. Jad was so self-contained I hadn't thought at first of how all this might affect him. Not only losing his position, so to speak, his right to lead, his reason for being with us, but also having no mate. The man was lonely. I came to recognize this all the more as time passed.

I would assume there were homosexual Neanderthal men somewhere out there but the likelihood of bumping into one seemed exceedingly slight. Jad was going to be alone.

Indeed, the likelihood of bumping into other humans at all did not seem strong. We had been told of it happening. We had seen no one, thus far. The tribes were surely small and scattered. This contributed to the slow tool development of that age. There wasn't a big enough population, not enough skilled craftsmen to support trade. New ideas did not spread quickly, and it might be assumed some never did. Many innovations might have died with their innovators or been carried on by their tribes for a generation or two before disappearing into inchoate prehistory.

Who could guess what might become of any new ideas we might contribute? "We could create a Neanderthal renaissance," I joked once. "Here in Sixty thousand BC."

"Fifty-seven Seventy-four, to be exact," Blackbird informed me. "It's a pretty good time. The world has been warming up for a few thousand years after one of the deeper glaciations and will continue to for a while."

"Not warmed up enough," groused Condor. That was something with which we could all agree. It was the Ice Age and it was cold, even in Italy, even in summer. Even in an alleged warm spell.

"Then we need to stock up on more food so we needn't leave the cave all winter," I announced. "It is time for some serious hunting."

The four of us were sitting apart. That was becoming the norm; Jad and Blackbird and Condor and me conferring, while Raven was more likely to be with Fat Bear. Spear Thrower too. I rose and turned to those three now.

"Hunt go on, um, day come sun, sun," I told them in my best Neanderthal. I pointed toward the north. "That is supposed to mean the day after tomorrow," I added in English. "If you want to come." We would need a day to prepare and plan. The women deserved warning ahead of time too.

* * *

The women—I would spend the rest of my life with them. They were my tribe, from Spruce Tree down to Acorn and the other little ones. Let me name them to you now, as I had come to know them. Let me show them, standing about the flickering dung fire in that cave, as they were an age ago, long before you and I were born.

Dusk Light, Spear Maker's mother, was the tallest. She was not as deep chested as most but had a heavy brow and large, somewhat pointed nose. She was pale but not freckled much, and her hair came close to being red. Dusk Light's sister, She Bear, had similar skin tone and hair, and perhaps an equally large nose, but was shorter and stockier—more barrel-like.

Spruce Tree, too, was thickly built, big-boned, but with regular, almost 'handsome' features. Their effect was sometimes spoiled a bit by her tendency to absent stares that made her look a bit mindless. Never believe that—there were wheels turning. Turning slowly, maybe, and not actually wheels. Those hadn't been invented yet! Her hair was the typical reddish-brown, not too dark, and she tanned well but some freckles were visible. The eyes were fairly light, in the hazel-green range.

Last Star had black hair—or dark brown really—but with the typical sun lightening. She was somewhat stocky and big-boned like her mother, Spruce Tree, but with a longer face and heavier jaw, and quite a lot of freckles. The eyes were a hazel-gray.

Little Rabbit resembled Last Star somewhat but had reddish hair. I knew that might darken as she matured and she would probably look all the more like her cousin. She was not as stocky as either Last Star or her aunt. The girl freckled more than tanned and her eyes were relatively dark.

Wolf Chaser, as I've mentioned, tanned the darkest, but her hair looked almost blond from the sun. She had heavier brows and a flatter, but still large, nose, with eyes of blue-gray. Of course, I thought her the most beautiful of the tribe. Who knows? Maybe I was right.

# 20.

THOSE WOMEN MADE SURE all the menfolk understood they were expected to turn out for the hunt. They might have just wanted to be rid of us a while, out from underfoot.

I think only Raven resented it. He had become independent of the rest of us, more interested in tramping about on his own, setting his snares, hunting small game. Sometimes Spear Maker was his companion; as often he was solitary.

The pale predawn light greeted us. "We'd best enjoy these early mornings while we can," spoke Jad. "We're past the midsummer now."

"It might have been nice to celebrate it somehow," Raven said. "I'll admit, I've lost track of the date."

"There is no date here," I told him, and pointed eastward. "We hunt across the hills today."

"Damn," muttered Fat Bear. "Couldn't we stick to flat land?"

"I want to know what lies that way. Best we do it as a group." I wouldn't have felt safe exploring on my own, though I might have chanced it. Best to have these men with me.

"I am as much on the outlook for resources as meat," I went on. "Nuts and fruits. And we need a source of workable stone. Maybe some decent wood. Keep an eye open for anything useful."

The Bear complained further. "We'd be better off looking where we know there is game."

"Next time." I took off and they followed. Fat Bear held off on grousing for a while. Climbing the slope took too much breath and effort. It was not a particularly steep slope, mostly open land, the trees few and stunted save in gullies where small streams flowed. I eyed the hazelnuts we had seen there before. It was too soon for the nuts yet. In time.

* * *

On our last crossing over the ridge, the hunt where I had taken the ibex, we had traveled south of the cave. We had gone north before turning this time. There was no narrow valley awaiting us here but a vista of rolling, heather-clad hills. There might be higher land beyond, mountains even. Mists, pearl and pale gold in the light of the rising sun, lay on the lowlands. And what was that shimmering far off there?

I pointed toward it. It was Raven who said, "I think that is a lake."

"Maybe so," agreed Jad. "I've not gone this way before and the other expedition never reported it. The first expedition, that is. I led those that followed. But there are lakes in the area now." An abashed chuckle, a shake of the head. "I mean sixty thousand years from now."

Condor said, "I know Trasimeno but we should be nowhere near there."

"This one doesn't look that big," I said. "It also looks pretty far away. Want to go look at it?"

"We're voting?" asked Fat Bear. There was a bit of a snicker attached.

And my brusque reply might have been triggered by it. "No, I'm asking for your thoughts." I turned to Spear Maker. "Big

151

water hills." I pointed in the lake's direction. "Spear Maker, um, go?"

The boy gave me a blank look. My Neanderthal was not proving sufficient. Jad stepped in and the two jabbered at each other for a while. Some of it I understood. "Spear Maker knows nothing of a lake," Jad informed us at last. "The tribe has no word for it. He does think it is too far."

I nodded. I made it a slow and thoughtful nod. "Yeah, we'll save it for some other time. Let's follow this valley south." It was barely a valley at all. We encountered no streams as we descended the slope, nor at its bottom. We saw no animals. Just rolling empty hills.

Not really empty. I knew they were alive under the grasses and heathers. The musics of bird and insect filled the crystalline air. There would be small furtive mammals all about us.

"Hold up," called Raven. He and Spear Maker were bent over, examining the ground. "Something big has been through here. Our mammoth, I'd bet." He rose and pointed. "Headed off that way." The boy blinked in agreement.

"That's toward the lake," remarked Condor.

"Might be a place he likes to hang around." If the young bull was similar in his habits to elephants he'd enjoy visiting a water hole. Could he be ambushed? Could we be up to it?

That was something to consider some other time. "Let's head for those rocks," I said. An outcropping rose some distance ahead. Our path along the bottom of the valley slightly sloped down toward it, ending at its foot. We would have to turn to one side or the other there to progress further, cross back over to our valley or climb the slope to the right to see what lay beyond.

It was as tall a cliff as any we had come across, rising maybe ten or twelve meters above us. Meters weren't a useful unit of measurement anymore, were they? Feet would be better. We all had feet with which to measure things. So nearly forty feet, smooth and sheer, of pale limestone. Water seeped from it near the base, making the ground moist but insufficient to form more than a puddle.

"I think we are somewhat opposite our cavern here," spoke Raven. "Just over this ridge."

Jad nodded. "That's possible. We should explore it further sometime."

I recalled there seemed to be airflow through that cavern. Maybe there was an opening to it somewhere over this way. That, too, was something to explore later. I was ready to move on when Spear Maker pointed upward and spouted a torrent of excited words. I couldn't make much sense of them.

Jad looked puzzled too, and told the young man he didn't understand.

"Bzzzz. Bzzz!" the boy went and eagerly pointed again. He licked his lips.

"I do believe that's a bee hive up there," said Condor. "And I do not think I can climb this cliff."

"Wild honey," breathed Fat Bear. "I would kill for something sweet."

"They might kill you first," Jad told him, "though I know none of you have an allergy to bee stings. You wouldn't have been permitted to come." He peered up at the nest—essentially a vertical crack in the cliff face with bees coming and going. Gathering nectar while they could. "It would be hard to get at them and dangerous if we could."

"Smoke, maybe?" asked Raven. He'd probably read something about beekeeping at some time.

"Cold," I said. "We can wait for a chilly morning when the little girls are sluggish."

"And dangle a line from above," said Jad, nodding. "Maybe we should go up and look around."

I agreed. "Easier to climb to the right, there." The cliff merged into a gentle grassy slope. Further ahead, a few lower escarpments could be spied rising from the green, We reached a low ridge and looked back into the blind valley we had left—an oblong bowl set among the hills. "I have no doubt larger game passes through here sometimes," I said. "Deer or horses maybe. They might go for water at that lake. There is a great deal we have to learn yet." I almost added 'before winter' but thought better of it. Worrying about what was to come would help nothing.

We were heading along the ridge line toward our cliff now. "It wouldn't hurt to put a lookout up here to watch what comes and goes," said Jad. "We could take turns."

"And you're going to make a schedule for us?" grunted Fat Bear.

"If you wish," was all our former guide was willing to say.

There was a fair amount of hill rising behind our cliff when we reached its top. Jad stepped out and looked down the sheer face. I wasn't willing to get that close to the edge. Maybe if I had a rope tied to me. "The fall would probably kill one," he remarked. "Hmm, a few bees, aren't there?"

Not a lot but I did notice them in the air around us. "Best not to linger," I said. "Onward and upward."

"I could set some more snares over here," spoke Raven, as we climbed. "Should move them around from area to area."

"Good idea," said Fat Bear. "You're doing a great job. Bringing in more meat than anyone else."

Which was true, up until the moment we brought home a large kill. I hoped today would bring that moment. We worked our way to the top of the wide, rounded ridge and looked out over our own familiar valley, our stream below us but mostly concealed by the willows. "That's our pond, right?" asked Condor, pointing.

I nodded, and surveyed the scene. "Horses over there," I said. "Across the stream and to the north." Not that far from the pond, and headed out of the more forested area beyond it. "Maybe the herd we tried to chase before. Too far away now."

"Our cavern should be close, then," said Jad. "Off to our left some."

"Yeah. Shh." I crouched and trusted the others to follow my lead.

Raven crouched beside me. "Red deer, wasn't it?"

"Think so." It didn't seem to have noted us, though I could not see it well from this vantage. "Where's the wind?" I whispered, mostly to myself.

"North. We're downwind."

Good. "Raven, Spear Maker, with me. The rest of you try to work closer while we circle around."

"We should spread out a little," Jad informed the others. "Bear to my right, Condor to my left." He couldn't help taking charge, I suppose, and maybe there was a need for it. Fat Bear definitely scowled but did as directed.

Having had my spear thrower slip out of my hand the first time I had hunted with it, I had added a loop of twisted fiber to go around my wrist. It made it easier to carry, too. My spear rested in it now, ready for action, as I crept along through the high heather. I wanted to get at least above the deer and maybe beyond it, without getting upwind. We could spread out when we got closer.

Raven had his spear and thrower ready too, in his left hand. None of the Neanderthals were left-handed. They were amazed that Raven favored his left hand when they finally noticed. The whole tribe had watched him for a couple days until the novelty wore off.

I motioned for Spear Maker to hold position when we got just above the grazing beast. It seemed quite oblivious. A stag it was, the antlers still in velvet of course and not very large. Perhaps only a yearling. Young anyway. This was a good spot for me to approach. "You move a little further down slope," I whispered to Raven. "Not to where the wind will warn him." With any fortune

—and some skill, maybe—the three of us would get a spear into him and our other hunters would not need to become involved.

The stag raised his head, sniffed the air. Had the wind changed? I continued to work toward him, trusting the others to do the same. The head went down. Up again. Was I close enough for a cast? The angle wasn't good.

Spear Maker rose and launched his missile. He was in best position. Raven and I at once jumped up to throw also. I had nothing but tail to aim at and managed to miss that. Raven connected but his spear did not penetrate well and fell out as the deer bounded away from us.

But Spear Maker's shaft protruded from its side. He had struck well. Deep enough to be mortal? We would find out. I scooped up my spear as I ran after it, noting that our other hunters had risen up ahead of the fleeing animal, ready to launch their own spears. None seemed to connect. More practice when we got back to the cave! The stag veered away and back toward me. Directly toward me. I think it had decided running me over was the best way to escape.

Should I attempt a cast? Or stand my ground and attempt to stab at it? I didn't have to decide. It's knees buckled as it approached and it fell practically at my feet. I jabbed into its side to be certain but Spear Maker's throw had brought it down.

The lad would be insufferable.

# 21.

"THIS IS PERHAPS A larger than normal tribe, especially with our addition. There is some evidence that smaller family groups lived in proximity to each other and occasionally came together to share, to socialize, to hunt."

"And find mates, I'd guess."

Blackbird smiled at that. "Yes. There was always some gene flow, among the Neanderthals themselves, of course, and even between the ancestors of we moderns and the Neanderthals. The Denisovans too. There was obviously cultural flow; the tools they used indicate that. It takes people to carry ideas from one place to another and when people meet other people there is likely to be sex."

"Yeah." I sat and thought a little before going on. "Do you think we'll have kids? I've heard different theories on, um, the fertility question."

"We're absolutely certain, from the genetic record, that Neanderthals and moderns did have healthy, fertile descendants. We have the proof in our own DNA. Whether all those descendants were without problems is more iffy. I suspect we will find out."

"Ha, but there will be no scientific journal to publish our research."

"That won't keep you from experimenting, I am sure." She paused, frowned slightly, continued. "It is possible we and the Neanderthals are a so-called ring species. Problems with fertility might have showed up when later, more advanced moderns—like ourselves—came up against the late Western European Neanderthals. Problems that didn't arise when early moderns met Neanderthals in the Near East. There may have been mixing there over hundreds of thousands of years."

"Early moderns, huh? They're in the Middle East now, right? North Africa too. I wonder what they're like."

"I wouldn't be at all surprised if they looked somewhat like aboriginal Australians. Maybe later waves were more similar to the Khoisan people. The bushmen, you know? There hasn't been any time-travel expedition to check that out yet." Blackbird shrugged and looked out over the valley. "And we'll never learn unless we mount our own expedition."

"Maybe later." I joked when I said it but I recognized there was a serious element to all this. What if there were no births here? We would be doing these women, this tribe, a disservice if there were none to carry on after us. Better they find Neanderthal males and we move on, if we proved to be incompatible.

And where else but across the strait to North Africa? That was something for the future. No need to worry about it now. Our immediate survival was more important.

"Yes, later." She seemed to muse on that for a moment before brightening to her normal self. "But right now I should let you get back to Wolf Chaser. She is giving me unfriendly looks."

Maybe I did spend too much time in the company of Kat-turned-Blackbird. No one else could provide the serious conversation she did—and perhaps I did the same for her. There was never a suggestion of more, though I think my mate and the other women would not have disapproved. It was just being ignored that bothered Wolf Chaser.

Therefor, I asked her to accompany me on my exploration of the morning. I wanted to check on those hazel thickets, mark them out, see how the nuts were coming along. I was also thinking of cutting some for their wood. Hazel wands should be at least as useful as willow. I would wait until autumn, after we gathered the nuts, for that.

Wolf Chaser did the gatherer thing as we went, although I shirked the hunter half of that proposition. I found myself carrying a fair amount of nut grass when we headed back to the cave, before midday. Also some tuberous objects that I suspected were a wild radish. I depended wholly on my young mate to recognize what was edible.

* * *

We returned to turmoil. "There was an altercation between Jad and Fat Bear," reported Raven.

"Physical?"

He shrugged. "Neither looks damaged."

Both men were present and both seemed intact. They were avoiding looking at each other. Blackbird was in conference with the other women, at the mouth of the cave. I decided not to get involved. Yet. Who might know whether it would become necessary?

I spied Spear Thrower and Condor coming up the slope and went to meet them. "You hear what happened?" was Condor's greeting.

I shook my head. "Only that there was some sort of, um, disagreement."

"More than that. Yukey took a swing at Jad but didn't connect. They might have gone at it but we showed up. Spear Thrower and me was down there catching these little guys." Condor grinned as he held up a string of rather tiny silvery fish. "I invented a fish spear for us." He then held up the primitive pronged stick in his other hand. So did Spear Thrower.

"What was the problem?" I asked, falling in beside them.

"Yukey was giving Blackbird unwanted attention. More than that, I guess. It set off Jad." He frowned and spat on the ground. "Damn, it would've set me off too."

The two men had moved closer together. Jad eyed Fat Bear with mingled caution and distaste. The Bear turned to us. "He wants to keep Kat from having a mate and use her as a bargaining chip to control us," he claimed. "It's not like the pansy has any use for her himself."

Condor's eyebrows raised at this but Raven appeared less surprised. I guessed Fat Bear had mentioned it to him before. How Fat Bear knew of it I couldn't say. Maybe he had our guide investigated before we came here.

All this was in English so our tribe, our women, had no idea what Fat Bear had said.

"If I did choose a new mate, it wouldn't be you, Bear," stated Blackbird, stepping forward from the knot of women. This she said in the dialect of the Neanderthals, so they would understand it fully. There might have been a smirk or two.

Fat Bear looked about and apparently decided there was no point in further bluster. He turned and strode away from us. "That won't be the end of that," Condor noted.

That was for certain. Once he had started in, the Bear was not going to let up. "Jad wants to run everything here," he confided to anyone who would listen, and, "Jad would just as soon the rest of us die so he can survive." I didn't take him seriously but maybe I should have. The women seemed uncertain. Even Raven seemed willing to listen to his rants.

Fat Bear did not call attention to himself again nor call out Jad publicly. I knew the feud simmered. We all did. But things seemed to settle down over the next couple days, and things went on.

# 22.

"I KNOW MODERN UMBRIA better than Jad. I've even visited this cave and other sites." Blackbird looked up at Condor. "You've been in the area too, haven't you?"

He settled down beside us. "Just as a tourist. My wife and I made the pilgrimage to Rome a few years back and saw most of the sights while we were at it. Assisi. That might have been our closest stop."

"Pretty far from here, at least on foot. We're not far north of where the Nera runs. Or will run. I'm sure some sort of river must be there now. We'd have to cross a narrow bit of high land."

"Rivers can move quite a bit in sixty thousand years," I observed.

"But mountains don't and rivers have to run around them. I would not expect most of the lakes of the central Italy we knew to exist now."

"We'll have to go look closer at that lake we spied," said Condor.

"Yes, and go back for that honey too, when it's cooler. We might be able to combine those two expeditions." I would suggest it sometime to the others. "But tomorrow, the cavern. Are you coming, Condor?"

"Yeah. Raven says he'll stay and keep Spear Maker out of mischief. He's peeved you're not taking him along."

I'd decided not to, not this time. Or I advised Jad and the others not to include the boy. I was not in charge of this expedition even if I had largely planned it.

"By the way," Condor continued, "did you know the Bear is now whispering that Jad wants to bugger Spear Maker?"

"Who the hell would believe that?" snapped Blackbird.

"Repeat a lie enough times and people will start to believe." Condor waved an arm at the tribe, scattered about the cave. "These ones do not know anything about his sort. I know him too well. Well enough to take him seriously." His eyes lit on Dusk Light. "I'd best make a pilgrimage with my current wife," he said. "Off to bed."

I rose as he did. I should be with my own wife. Wife—I think I had avoided thinking of Wolf Chaser as such, naming her so in my mind. But wife she was; we had as strong a bond, as much of a social contract, as ever I had with the wife of that other life. And this one might last better.

* * *

We did not hurry away the next morning. There was no need. The plan was to explore deeper into our cavern, more to satisfy our own curiosity than anything else. Yes, too, we could see if there was anything of value there. It might serve as a place of refuge, if needed, or as a store room. Things might keep well in its cold depths.

Those depths might also harbor the dens of animals. That is, animals other than the bats who housed themselves in the first chamber. I somewhat doubted this, at least at this time of year; it might be an attractive hibernation choice for a bear in a few months. One could probably squeeze through the entry.

Jad led, with the unspoken consent of Condor and myself.

What Fat Bear thought of it we did not ask. It was as warm a morning as any we had known here. That, we all knew, would not last. I, at least, felt an urgency to prepare for the coming winter.

But then, I'm a born worrier, as more than one friend or relative has informed me over the years. It stood me in good stead in business. Not so much in life.

Mid-morn found us sliding into darkness. We had plenty of rope with us this time, twisted of a mix of plant and animal fiber. The Neanderthals knew nothing of braiding and teaching them was not a priority at the moment. Maybe come winter. So our lines typically consisted of three strands of fibers twisted one direction and tied off, and then three of those ropes twisted together in the opposite direction. More was unnecessary; they seemed of adequate strength. Maybe if I were dangling over a cliff gathering honey I'd want something more.

We had equipped ourselves well with torches as well. Condor held his high and surveyed the roof. "I saw young ones clinging to their mothers the last time. Maybe they're all grown up now."

I peered upward, not that there was much to see. I certainly hadn't noticed any babies before but I hadn't been looking for them. "I suppose they need to mature quickly, before they have to sleep through the winter."

"I wouldn't be surprised if they went deeper into the cave for hibernation," said Jad. "Maybe we'll see droppings further on and find out."

"They wouldn't poop much while they slept," Condor pointed out.

"Let's hope bat droppings are the only kind we come across," muttered Bear.

We filed into the next room, following the depression created by trickling water. I hoped there were pools further down; a water source would make these caverns more useful if we were ever forced to inhabit them. It would be unlikely to freeze, down deep, but it might not be replenished when all the water was solid in the outside world.

There was water in this next chamber, to be sure, tiny puddles here and there. Damp places on the floor might be a better description. An occasional drip fell from one of the stalactites. They were surprisingly loud here in this still, dark underground world. The roof lowered into blackness ahead of us.

Jad held his torch low. "There is water flow through here too," he stated. "It doesn't end in this room."

Yes, there was a shallow meandering depression leading toward the other side of the space. I glimpsed no sign of bat guano—or signs of any animal life—anywhere. This was all limestone, floor, walls, ceiling, as far as I could tell. We proceeded toward what we assumed was a passage.

"Too damn damp here," said Fat Bear.

"It is," Jad agreed. "And bat-ridden too. I couldn't see using it save as a place of temporary refuge."

"Which we might need someday," I said. "That's a low roof." A dark hole, wide enough but no more than three feet high, gave entry to whatever mysteries lay beyond.

Jad only nodded, crouched and led the way in. The floor was definitely wet through this passage. And slippery.

"Good place to run into a bear," commented Condor.

"Yeah. Hey!" I heard a crash ahead of me, saw a torch swing, Two torches. One went out. "Damn, I landed on my fat ass," spoke the Bear.

"And knocked Jad down," said Condor. "Either of you hurt?" The three had been little better than silhouettes to me, bringing up the rear of our column and, like the others, sidling in a bent over posture.

"Okay," I hear Jad call. "I slid down a slope, I think, and lost my light."

"And I slid down on top him," added Fat Bear.

I crept forward carefully. I didn't wish to add to the pileup. Condor was sitting at the edge of a downward turn in the passageway. "It's not steep," he said, turning to me as I crouched beside him. "Just slippery."

I looked toward the torch light ahead. "Not very far either. But maybe I should tie a line here."

"To what?" He held his flame high. "Nothing but smooth rock. Hey, Bear Man, do you think you can climb back up?"

"Will see." A moment later Fat Bear pulled himself up beside us. "Just got to stay close to the wall. It's slick down the middle."

"Okay. Jad, we're coming on down to you," I called. I could see only the torch glimmering. Two torches now. He must have found the dropped one and reignited it. Fat Bear took it without comment when we came together again at the bottom.

We could stand upright there. It was still a passage, a tunnel, but roomier. We weren't really very deep into this cavern yet and had no idea how far it might extend into the limestone underlying the hills. Nor how deep it might go.

"Maybe we should all be tied together," I suggested, holding up a length of rope. None of them seemed enthusiastic about the idea.

"If we reach a steep spot," said Jad. The other two said nothing, so I let it go.

"I feel air moving," Condor noted.

"Water's moving too," said Fat Bear. "This trickle is turning into a stream."

Technically, yes, one could have called it a stream. All the little leaks and trickles were coming together, flowing from one shallow puddle to another, slowly moving forward and down-ward. As were we.

Jad held up a hand to halt. "What's that sound?"

It wasn't loud. "Falling water?" I hazarded.

"I think so. Be careful moving forward." A minute later we emerged into a larger space, a high-domed room, and a little off-center yawned a pit. Not a large pit, maybe six or eight feet across. A hole in the cave floor and into that hole flowed the trickle that had accompanied us here, into the bowels of the earth, to use a well-worn cliché.

By the flickering light, I could see the room was roughly

circular and appeared to have no other exits. And— "Is there a draft in here?"

"I think so," said Jad. "Up there." He pointed to a spot above the pit. Yes, the smoke from our torches was wafting toward some unknown outlet above.

"We aren't on the other side of the ridge, are we?" asked Condor.

Fat Bear snickered. "Nah, we haven't gone anywhere near that far. We'd haveta walk miles to go all the way through the hill."

A pretty good distance, at least. But the water going into this hole might just seep out over there somewhere. Maybe even at the base of the bee cliff, which I was sure was quite a bit lower than where we stood. I carefully made my way closer to that dark pit. I could see no bottom. "I think we've reached the end of our underground road," I said.

"Let's go all the way around the walls and make certain," said Jad. He went to the left and Fat Bear followed. Condor and I went the other way. By the time we were on opposite sides of the room all we could see of each other were our torches in the darkness. I didn't much like that darkness and was altogether ready to climb back out of it.

A shout, just a short exclamation—it might have been 'whoa!'—and then silence. I looked across the cave to see only one light.

"Jad fell!" cried out Fat Bear. "Fell into that goddamn hole!"

# 23.

I SLID AS CLOSE as I dared. I could see nothing. Jad had disappeared into those dark depths. "Jad!" I called out. "Can you hear me?" My companions added their voices but no answer came.

Condor crouched just behind me, keeping a grip on my ankle as I inched closer. He looked up at Fat Bear. "What happened?" His voice was flat.

"Jad was leading the way. It got narrower over there." He gestured toward the far side of the pit. "And slippery too, I guess. 'Fore I knew it, he slipped and—and went in."

"Hmm." There was something in the tone of that 'hmm' but I didn't have time to think about it.

"Do you think you two can lower me in?" There was no question that I was going down that hole. As far as I could.

"Do you think that's a good idea?" Condor's voice came almost as a whisper. "With an untested line and just the two of us up here?"

"We'll use two ropes." We had certainly brought enough. I had made certain of that. "One of you on each line." I shortly had two lines fastened around my torso and took up one of the torches. The other two were jammed into rocks near by. Fat Bear and Condor each took a rope and a moment later I had gone over the edge, into a pit that was, as far as I knew, bottomless.

Had I taken even a moment to think of it, I might not have trusted my life to those twisted strands of fiber and the two not-exactly-young men slowly playing them out. I hoped with all my being they were not allowing them to fray against the rock lip!

One hand held the torch; with the other, and my feet, I attempted to keep a firm contact with the wall. It sloped ever so slightly, which was to my advantage.

It was also rather slick, which was not. I held my torch out and peered downward but could still see nothing. My thoughts went to Condor. There had been, what, incredulity in his voice? Veiled but maybe there. Did he mistrust Fat Bear's account of what had happened? This was not the time to be worrying about that, especially with Fat Bear holding one of my lifelines.

Condor's voice wafted down to me. It sounded surprisingly far away. "That's far enough," he called. "We won't chance letting out more line."

Then I had gone down pretty far. I again looked into the depths below. "I see his body," I called, my voice echoing and reechoing from the walls around me. "There is no way he is alive and I can't reach him. We could come back later with a longer line."

No, there was definitely no way he was alive. Jad had fallen far and onto rock. I had held onto a hope there would be a pool of water at the bottom of the shaft. That would have been the only way the man could have survived. "Pull me up."

I didn't like to think on what I had seen but there was nothing else to occupy my thoughts as I was slowly dragged upward. How did our Neanderthals deal with the death of one of their tribe? None had died during our time here. Blackbird would know or be able to ask. Then I was over the edge, arms assisting me onto the cave floor. I dropped my torch, not caring whether it went out. I was a little surprised I had clutched it all the way up.

"He's broken," I reported. I hadn't been able to make out much detail but from the angle of his head I knew Jad's neck had been snapped. "We should come back for the body. Maybe tomorrow."

"Then let's get out of here," said Fat Bear. We wound our way back through the passages and chambers. Our spears we had left with the bats. I gathered Jad's up with my own. Maybe someone could use it. There was little talk on the way back.

\* \* \*

Jadunath Palit—a different Jad lived in the world from which we had come, a Jad who was unaware this one had ever existed and died sixty thousand years before he was born. I hoped that Jad's life was good. "Let me tell Blackbird first," I told the others. "Then we'll see about breaking it to everyone else."

"They'll see Jad isn't with us," Condor reminded me.

Yes, they would. "No one will think anything of it for a while." A few minutes later we spied our cave, as we had left it that morning. All seemed peaceful. It was only mid-afternoon. Clouds had gathered since we left, adding more gloom to the day. I expected rain later.

That was good. This day needed to be washed away. Blackbird was seated at the mouth of the cave, working on something. No, she was only filing her nails. The little pieces of sandstone in our tool kits for smoothing wood were also useful for this. I do not know if any of our Neanderthals had followed this practice before we arrived but several had picked it up since.

172

I sat down beside her and gave it to her bluntly. "Jad is dead. He had a fall."

She swore soundlessly and stared at the lump of stone in her hand for a few seconds. "We should tell Spruce Tree first," she said. "If only to acknowledge her position here."

It made sense to let her in before telling the rest of the tribe. Blackbird rose. "Let's go find her. She should be down at the stream."

"Okay." We walked, side by side, down the slope. "Would you like to have this?" I asked after a while, holding out Jad's spear. She nodded and took it without comment.

"Do you know what the customs are here for, um, dealing with death? Burial?"

"This tribe has no customs. Bodies are deposited somewhere well away from the cave and that's it."

"So none of the cave burials we've read about?"

She shook her head.

"Where Jad is now might be as good a cave burial as any," I said, as much to myself as to Blackbird. She had asked nothing about the circumstances of his death.

"So he fell in this cavern of yours?"

"Yes, into a pit." Should I say more? "I think Condor suspects Fat Bear of pushing him. I think maybe I do too." I might not have till just that moment. When I put it into words it seemed more believable.

A quick intake of breath. "But you didn't see it?"

"No." I could tell what I knew of what happened in the dark

later. We found Spruce Tree among the willows. She held a nest full of eggs—quite possibly blackbird eggs.

"I should admonish her about disrespecting my totem," whispered my companion, giving me only the slightest of smiles. Instead we greeted the tribal elder and told her of our tragedy, I saying as much as Blackbird. I was not as fluent, and never would be, but I could manage the dialect enough to be understood now. Understanding what others said to me was not quite so far along.

Be that as it may, it behooved me to give most of the account of how Jad's death happened. I made no mention of Fat Bear's possible role.

Spruce Tree listened placidly to it all, blinked to express her understanding at the conclusion, and began to wail. Women and children began to appear. They added to her lamentations as soon as they learned what had occurred. It must have been customary to express grief so. That was all I could figure.

They all stopped pretty much as one, though I suspect Spruce Tree cued it. She led the group toward the cave, marching stolidly up the heather-clad slope. Not a word was spoken. It may be noted that the Neanderthals had a certain lack of expressiveness in their features at all times. They don't have as much control over their facial muscles as we moderns, or so I had been told. The simple lifting of an eyebrow, something we hardly think of, was not often seen.

But they felt as deeply as you and I. This I never had reason to doubt.

No formal announcement was needed. Word of Jad's demise

spread rapidly among those not already in the know. I assumed one of the men had already told Raven. And I let Condor tell the story to those who wanted it. He was better with the language.

Though Jad had denied holding any authority, we had looked to him for leadership. This was among the thoughts I could not dismiss, through the evening and later when I tried to sleep. Who now? Spruce Tree, to be sure, remained but she was not the one to initiate anything. Would that Blackbird could take charge, but the tribe would not follow her.

And what of Fat Bear? Did he murder Jad in the darkness of that cavern? We could never be certain. I was certain he would attempt to assert himself now. Assert himself more. As might Condor—and myself, for that matter. We were three highly competitive and highly successful businessmen. It was to be expected we would butt heads, with each other and with anyone else who tried to rein us in.

Ah, I could only wait and see how things went. Tonight, it was comforting to know I was safe with my tribe, that my woman lay beside me. The future need not be bleak. I fell asleep making plans for the next day.

We must bring Jad back to the tribe.

# 24.

FAT BEAR REMAINED BEHIND this time. That was his decision. "I'm not in good enough condition to do that two days in a row," he claimed, and maybe he was right. I was willing to leave him at the cave.

Condor and I were joined by Spear Maker and Raven. Now that we'd scouted out the further reaches of the caverns I was completely willing to have the young Neanderthal with us. I do not think he entirely understood why we would return for a dead man but he raised no objections.

Storm had raged through the night, the wind rushing and howling down the valley. It blew this morning too, brisk and cool from the north. "The first touch of the winter to come," Blackbird had said. I would have wanted her along with us but she refused. "Show me the cave some other time and don't let Spear Maker know about it. He believes it is a sacred place for men."

"Oh, the club house for the He-Man Woman-Haters. Good enough." With that we had hiked away on our errand. What would we do with Jad's remains, assuming we could get them out of that hole? Bring them back to the cave or bury them some-where? Or even lay them to rest in that chamber. I just didn't want to leave them where they were.

A sacred place for men. It hadn't been our intent to make Spear Maker believe that but I could see how it had happened. If we ever needed the cave for some other purpose we would have to disabuse him of the idea. Maybe it *could* be used as a graveyard of sorts. For men only? Ah, there were more important things to which I should turn my thoughts and intentions. Bilberry season was upon us. Not many of those grew along the higher path we followed along the hillsides this morning but they were thick on lower ground. The women and children were already out picking them. I did trust Fat Bear to keep a watch over them but I would feel better when all of us were together.

When that season ended we must seriously hunt. Then followed the ripening of acorns, and of hazelnuts, and undoubtedly other foodstuffs of which I was completely unaware. For this, I trusted—and must trust—Spruce Tree and the other adult women.

Eventually, too, we would see the grazing animals migrating southward. Reindeer. Those were the most important, I suspected, but there were surely other species on the move as the seasons changed. The mammoths. I couldn't forget those.

* * *

No animals showed themselves this morning, nor did we dawdle or stop for anything on our way. The sun was still low over the hills when we arrived at the cavern entrance. One by one, we lit our torches from a coal Spear Maker had carried, in dirt wrapped in a bit of hide. There was a little fat on the ends of our wooden torches to help them ignite. In we went, and past the sleeping bats. We must seem familiar to the little flying creatures by now.

On into the larger chamber we passed, the room where Spear Maker had undergone his initiation. He looked it over with a more discerning eye now, taking in the stalactites and stalagmites, the high ceiling disappearing into darkness, the damp floor. His eyes went to the low exit. "We go there?" he asked.

"That we do," Condor told him. "I'll lead the way. Keep close to the walls and avoid the slippery places."

The lad hesitated at the entrance. "Does Great Bear live here?" he asked. He was attempting to sound more calm than he felt, I thought.

"Not now," Raven informed him. "It's not time to sleep yet."

Spear Maker nodded his head. He'd picked that up from us. Crouching, he followed Condor into the passage.

"Great Bear?" I whispered to Raven as we went in after him.

"I've been told all about him," he replied. "Great Bear hibernates in a vast cavern far below the world and brings spring when he awakens. He is son and mate of Earth, who is mother to all."

"Oh." We sidled along for a few seconds. "Are there other gods?"

"I'm not certain. I haven't figured out the point of some of the stories I've been told. The sun and moon and maybe the stars have a meaning, but I don't know if they are gods as you and I know the word. There seems to be an animistic view of the world." He chuckled. It sounded odd in this space. "My main source is Rabbit so I'm not inclined to take any of it too seriously."

Little Rabbit would be entirely likely to make up anything she didn't know. She had the makings of a religious leader.

We emerged into the final room. Raven and Spear Maker were given time to fully survey it before I spoke. "Aside from that dangerous hole in the middle of the chamber," I said, nodding in its direction, "it wouldn't be a bad place to stay. In an emergency maybe."

"It's cold in here," complained Raven.

"But maybe no colder in winter. And it is dry." That was so. The water that ran into the room flowed straight to the shaft. "I'll go down," I announced. That seemed logical to me. I was lighter than Condor or Raven, and I wouldn't ask young Spear Maker to descend into that hole. "I may need to tie the line to Jad—to the body and let you hoist it out."

I hoped it remained intact. It seemed doubtful anything would molest it where it lay. No one said a word against me going into the pit so we tied the lines around me, two again but longer, and down I went.

Neck craned downward, trying to make out the bottom somewhere below me, I felt something grab at me with sharp talons. I'm sure I yelled. Maybe like a little girl. It was just luck that I didn't drop the torch. I held it above my head, trying to make out what had hold of me. Ah.

"What's wrong?" someone called from above. "Are you all right?"

"Yeah," I called back. "Just a cave cricket." I flicked the four inch long insect off. There was unlikely to be anything worse down here. I didn't have any scare left in me if there was.

I could see there were more of them on the walls. They could not see me, I assumed, most likely being blind. Would they bother the body? I knew nothing of cave crickets eating habits but I didn't think they went for flesh. Even in the Pleistocene. Ha, saber-toothed cave crickets!

"I'm near the bottom," I yelled. There was standing water down here, but not much. Puddles rather than a pool. I looked at the wall all around but saw no outflow. The water must simply seep out through the porous rock or through cracks too small to notice. Then my focus went to Jad. The corpse was intact. I couldn't help shaking my head seeing him lying there, blue and broken. I couldn't help having tears in my eyes.

Ah, get to work, Ken. I undid the loops from my torso and wrapped them around the body. No difficulties there, aside from it being quite wet and me having to juggle my torch. There was no place to jam it into the smooth rocks. I cinched both lines beneath the arms and called out, "Hoist away!" I assisted the load into an upright position as it was pulled upward, and watched it fade into the gloom above.

Leaving me in the bottom of a damp pit with a single flickering torch. There were quite a few bones down here. Washed in? That would take something stronger than the current flow through the cave but I could see it happening. There was fur too, bodies that had resisted decomposition in the cold. Some had a veneer of limestone on them. That would take time. A bear over there, I was pretty sure. Maybe it fell in. Maybe bears did hibernate in here through the winter.

"We're sending the rope down," came a call. From whom, I couldn't tell. The echoes in this tube distorted the voices too much. A moment later, both ropes appeared above me. Someone had the sense to tie this end of the two together, loosely knotted. I got them around me as quickly as possible, holding the torch in my teeth this time, and called to be pulled up. I did not wish to stay down there any longer than possible. And I was glad we decided—I decided, really—not to leave Jad at the bottom of this pit.

I was near the top when there came a sudden lurch, and I fell back a few feet. There was yelling from above but I could not make out words. I was hanging a bit sideways. One of the lines must have snapped. I felt for them and, yes, one was dangling. "Everyone on this rope," someone commanded. Condor, I was fairly sure. "Careful now!"

Darned right they'd better be careful. A few seconds later I was crawling over the lip of that shaft. Arms pulled me away from it. "We need stronger ropes," I told them. My eyes went to Jad's form. He had been wrapped in a worn reindeer hide we had carried with us. "Let's get out of here."

# 25.

IT WAS RAVEN WHO suggested sky burial. "I reckon no one with my name should object to that," said Condor. So we carried Jad's remains to the top of one of the rocky escarpments, one no four-legged scavenger should be able to climb, and left him there, with a brief ceremony. Some of the women came, some did not.

As we descended, Blackbird handed Spear Maker the spear of our late guide. It seemed fitting. Fitting enough.

"Maybe this will become the custom," Raven conjectured.

"Future anthropologists would curse you if they knew you started such a custom," came Blackbird's rejoinder. "They much prefer cave burials. Now let's go pick berries."

That took much of everyone's attention for the next few days. The sheer number of bilberries was astounding. Most were dried for the winter.

"We might store these fresh in the cavern," I remarked to the others. I didn't think the crickets would eat them. Of course, if bears hibernated there, things would be different!

"They would mold," stated Fat Bear. "I learned about that kind of thing despite myself. My second wife was a chef."

Condor nodded. "I remember. Vegetarian restaurant, right?" He made a bit of a face.

There was no reason to let anyone know I'd been a vegetarian until this jaunt into the past. The Ken Sasaki now living in the future was likely to have resumed that lifestyle. It was a bit impractical here.

"When the berries run out I think we should go explore the area around that lake," I said. I thought it likely bilberries grew about it too. We should be aware of resources in the area.

"That's pretty far," Fat Bear allowed.

"Agreed. About as far from our home base as I'd be willing to venture in one day." As far as the woods and marsh where we had taken the elk. Maybe farther. We spoke no more of it but went back to our tasks as gatherers. Being a hunter could wait a little while.

It should not be assumed our suspicions of the Bear had dissipated. Condor, I am sure, thoroughly believed he had murdered Jad. I wasn't as certain but did think it entirely possible. So did Blackbird. I wondered if she had said anything of it to the other women.

We had been leery of mentioning the idea to Raven. He got along well with Fat Bear. He joked about him being his father in law, what with Last Star being the daughter of Spruce Tree. It did create ties between the two men.

He even hinted that Fat Bear should be acknowledged as our leader now. "Someone should make decisions," he said, but did not pursue it.

"That should be Spruce Tree," I had said to Condor, when we spoke of it later.

"But the Bear is dominating her," he answered, "in his usual fashion. She may do what he says when it comes to making a decision." Spruce Tree didn't really like making decisions anyway. We both knew that.

There was no doubt Fat Bear thought of himself as top man here. The 'alpha' male, to use a discredited term. He had probably thought of himself that way wherever he was, throughout his life —and felt threatened if there were any challenge to his dominance.

"He will try to bully anyone and everyone," Condor assured me. "He may think he has you cowed you into submission but I know better."

And I knew he had no chance of getting Condor to fall into line. My friend might have been a little more like Fat Bear than he cared to admit to himself. Condor used people too. He might not mind trying to use the Bear, playing along with him as long as it was to his advantage.

As to the others, it was hard to say. Certainly, Blackbird loathed the man. Dusk Light too, but she didn't show it so much now. Maybe she had simply accepted Fat Bear. Or maybe she and Condor laid plans against him while wrapped in their sleeping furs!

Yes, it had grown cool enough, some evenings, to want a cover. All those bodies in the cave did keep it fairly warm still. There would come a time when furs would be necessary. Soon, maybe. Sooner than I and the others were prepared for. We must hunt.

\* \* \*

It was a sound I had never heard before, a deep coughing somewhere in the darkness. It woke Wolf Chaser, who sat up beside me.

"A bear?" she wondered. The woman sounded doubtful of that. I was too. There was low murmuring all through the cave. Many had been awakened.

Then a roar challenged the night and I no longer had any doubts. "The lion," I whispered. I rose at once and went to the cave entry.

Undoubtedly the lion. The not particularly large leopards would not make such a sound. "It has wandered north," I said to Fat Bear, who sat on guard with one of the youngsters. Nut Grass, it was.

"The one you saw before?"

I but nodded. It seemed likely. I lingered at the entrance for some time. Others came and went, the younger curious, the older apprehensive. There were whispered exchanges. The nocturnal prowler gave no further sign of his presence, not a single cough, and most settled back into sleep. In time, I too returned to my bed and my Wolf Chaser.

She had to quiz me extensively, never having seen a lion herself. And I knew enough of her tongue now to answer most of her questions. "Then like a lynx but much bigger?" she asked.

"Much bigger. We would be as rabbits are to the lynx."

She shivered at that thought but then proclaimed, "We shall kill it and you can have its skin." And with that she rolled over and went back to sleep.

\* \* \*

There was no chance to kill it. The lion disappeared, not being heard—much less seen—again. It did cross my mind that the predator could have been the reason this tribe had not remained here, in that other time line. It might have been too much for a tribe with no men. It might prove too much for our tribe with men.

Two days later we set out to investigate that distant lake and the area around, off to the northeast of our home. Raven and Spear Maker accompanied me. We decided Condor and Fat Bear would be of more use at the cave.

I felt they would slow us down but never actually said so. They would probably have pointed out that I was almost as old as they were. But they were happy to remain and no one had to attempt to assert any authority. I would do that as soon as we set forth. When we hunted, I was in charge and everyone recognized that. For now.

At first light we set out. It was cool enough for me to wrap myself in a hide poncho. Raven had made up some sort of vest for himself from rabbit skin. Laced together, not sewn. The Neanderthals hadn't figured out fitted clothes and sewing yet. Maybe that was another technology we should introduce. There would be more than enough opportunity through the winter. We would spend a lot of time in the cave, I was certain.

Spear Maker felt no need for more than his usual hide kilt. I suspected even he would soon want to wrap up in furs.

Knowing the lay of the land a little better now, we proceeded down our valley and crossed the ridge beyond the hidden cavern, ending up above the bee cliff. We stood on that ridge and gazed out toward our lake. Too much mist clung to hill and valley to pinpoint it this early but we knew the direction and set forth. To be sure, we were also keeping an eye open for game. That was more important than exploration. If we made a good kill, the lake could wait till another day.

What a vista lay before us! That truly was a distant spur of the Apennines off to our right, to the southeast, burnished by the rising sun. The land lay more open the way we were headed, rolling, heather-clad hills as far as we could see. The terrain looked easy to traverse. I guessed it was no more than ten miles to the lake. I hoped it was less than that.

Across a gold-bathed grassy valley we went, fording a rivulet running north. It might join our stream further along or flow off another way entirely. There was no time to follow it and find out.

In the distance ahead lay higher hills. It was possible that the upper valley of the Tiber—the proto-Tiber—lay on the other side of them, where the river's course curved back southward. That assumed it followed a course at least similar to that of the Tiber of sixty thousand years future. It was not close. That might be a good hunting area but we would not learn this year.

"There," said Raven as we crested the next ridge. It looked close. Close enough.

Closer yet I could spy grazing animals. They might be deer but I could not tell at this distance. I did not doubt they saw us as well; we were unlikely to sneak up on one on the open hills. Those hills fell away toward the lake. "It's all one big valley," I said. "We could parallel that stream down there." It flowed at the foot of the gentle slope we descended, not half as wide as that which coursed through our own valley. This one I could probably jump across, at least here.

I was not surprised to find more bilberry bushes along the stream. Their fruit was mostly gone but we picked a few to eat as we traveled. There were no willow thickets here, just the narrow stream boisterously flowing between steep but low rocky walls. We followed it north and east. I had expected it to grow and widen but the flow remained constrained within its narrow banks.

"Rabbits," remarked Spear Maker. "Many many rabbits."

"A bit far afield to set our snares, maybe," replied Raven.

"We would camp," said the young Neanderthal. "Stay here two nights, three nights." I believe he liked the idea of an extended hunting trip. It was the sort of thing the lost men of his tribe did.

"Not a bad idea," I said. "It would have to be done it before it gets too cold. I think we may need to change our route ahead."

That we did. There was a low cliff, over which our stream fell. The limestone face stood but three or four foot, easy enough to clamber down, but at its base the ground became marshy. Our little creek spread out and disappeared into a maze of puddles and rivulets, reeds and willows.

And before us lay our destination, the lake. "It's not as big as I thought," were Raven's first words.

"The wetlands around it made it look larger at a distance." That was a guess but I figured it was probably true. "It's still good sized. Hey, is that our friendly neighborhood mammoth over there?"

Raven shielded his eyes, for the sun was behind the form. "Could be, but the tusks look larger."

Another bull? That shouldn't have been surprising. We might see troops of mammoth soon though I didn't know if they migrated this far south in large numbers. I could ask the women when we got back to the cave.

"Let's skirt around this area," I suggested. It was more than a suggestion really, for I hopped across our stream and started eastward along the top of the low cliff. I expected to be followed. The cliff itself subsided into a slope not far along our path and there appeared to be firmer ground at its bottom.

Still, plenty of reed-filled marsh lay out a little further. I could hear the songs of the blackbirds among them, saluting the mid-morning sun. This shone strong and warm now, clearing the mist and leading me to doff my cape. "There are bound to be water-fowl here," I told the others.

Spear Maker nodded wisely and rattled off the names of nearly a dozen varieties. It is to be noted that each had its own unique name. I wasn't sure if a generic term for 'duck' even existed in the language. Probably none wintered here but they would certainly pass through on their migrations; they, as the rabbits, should be hunted sooner rather than later.

We hiked along the lakeside, the soil soft beneath us and criss-crossed by a bewildering number of tracks. I hoped to circumnavigate the body of water before heading back. If we took any game in the process, all the better.

But I wouldn't get too close to the bulky mammoth over there, whether it was 'ours' or another. Here, too, there were berry bushes, on the slopes leading down to the lake. Next year we must come here earlier, maybe the whole tribe, camp for a few days and stock our larder.

Next year—there was no guarantee we would be in the area still, or even alive. But making plans costs nothing. "Another stream." I pointed it out though I am sure my companions saw it. Quite possibly before I did. It was wider than the rivulet we had followed down to the lake, and its mouth was choked with reeds and willows. "Let's go upstream a little to cross."

And get up a little higher again, to get a look at things before continuing. As we climbed the slight slope, Spear Maker suddenly stopped, pointing to the ground. "Look," he called.

There in the soft sand were the unmistakable footprints of a man.

# 26.

THEY WERE THE PRINTS of broad, bare feet, and obviously not made by any of us.

"We're not the only ones to visit this lake," said Raven.

"Duh," replied Spear Maker. He had been learning sarcasm, mostly from Blackbird, and took to it as well as any teenager. "One man," he added.

"Going the same way as us." There wasn't any reason to stand and stare at them longer. "Let's move on."

I wondered if the stranger had gone upstream to cross, as were we, but we saw no more signs before going over the stream ourselves. Through it, I should say; it was a shallow spot and easy to ford. The water felt warmer than I was used to in our own little river.

Were we apprehensive from there on? Perhaps. Certainly a little more cautious than before, not that we were careless in a land where we might be both hunter and hunted. We worked back down to the lake's margin, continuing our survey. We were headed north by now. More or less.

I could see no sign of the mammoth. Maybe it came down to drink or bathe in the early morning and then went off to forage somewhere. It was time we foraged some.

* * *

"If you spear anything, you'll have to eat it raw," I informed the pair. "I'm leery of starting a fire if there are other men around."

Raven frowned. "That seems over-cautious."

Spear Maker only said, "I don't mind raw." In truth, the Neanderthals consumed more raw meat than cooked.

The two had been aching to put a spear into one of the numerous rabbits or waterfowl. "We could carry something back with us," I continued, "but it is a pretty long journey. I'd say wait until we're on our way home. In the mean time, let's sit down and have some of what we brought with us."

That was dried meat, of course. Maybe I should introduce pemmican to our tribe. The dried berries could be incorporated. I had only a loose idea of how to make it but it shouldn't be too difficult, should it? We chewed on the jerky—I think it was from our giant elk—for a while. We would continue along the northern shore of the lake when done. It was even marshier over here.

Being marshy, there were plenty of mosquitoes. Biting flies too. Did malaria or yellow fever exist here? We were fortunate to have contracted no diseases so far. That was another reason to avoid contact with other humans.

There was a distant low-pitched sound. In this drowsy midday, I wasn't paying much attention to such things but sat there finishing my lunch. It grew louder and somewhat less easy to ignore. "Sounds like cows," I commented.

Raven stood up and surveyed the grass around us. "Over there. Aurochs. The herd's coming down to drink, I think."

And that they did, not far from us. I didn't intend to molest them and trusted them to ignore me. "Let's spear one!" whispered Spear Maker.

"Only if you carry it home on your shoulders," I replied. "We can come back and have a real hunt sometime."

"All of us?" asked Raven. He half-settled back onto the grass, craning his head occasionally to keep an eye on the prehistoric bison.

"The whole tribe, maybe. We could set up camp for a couple weeks and butcher everything on the spot."

He looked at me for a few seconds, his face without expression. It was hard to tell what was going on in the novelist's head. "Is that a decision you're going to make?"

"It's a decision the tribe would have to make. Maybe, um, over Spruce Tree's objections. She's not been keen on taking chances this past year according to the other women."

"She would be all right with it if Fat Bear approved."

Spear Maker jumped in. "Dusk Light would go."

"Your mother has disagreed with Spruce Tree about this sort of thing, hasn't she?"

"Uh-huh." He grinned. "Condor would too."

"I'll bet," said Raven, rising. "The herd's headed off. Ready to move on?"

* * *

There was no outflow from the lake, but we crossed a couple more small streams emptying into its basin. Then we headed home. I decided ten miles had been an overestimation of the distance. Seven or eight was more like it. Still a good hike, round-trip.

Even more so if we had a load of meat. Spear Maker did knock down a wading bird. A sort of crane, I think. We crudely field dressed it and carried it with us.

I think the boy cared more about the feathers than the meat. He went on about what he would do with them at the cave. Not surprisingly, he intended to give some to Blackbird—the stone age equivalent of chocolates and jewelry. I am sure it hadn't been lost on Spear Maker that she was now without a mate.

But he also was saying this one would go Dusk Light and this to Rabbit and on through pretty much everyone in the tribe. These people did share. They would not think of hoarding something for themselves.

"What's going on?" asked Raven, as we approached the cave. It was near dusk but a large group stood outside the entrance. Maybe the entire tribe. Occasionally a wailing note arose. Not for very long.

"Something's wrong," was the only answer I had. The group stolidly awaited us—or awaited a move from Spruce Tree.

It was she who stepped forward and announced, "The lion returned. He killed Moss."

# 27.

MOSS WAS A BOY of five or six, one of the orphaned children. The women had wailed enough by the time we got home; now they were ready to give us the story.

They and Condor. "From there it came," said Spruce Tree, pointing south. Rocky terrain that direction would have given it cover. "It pounced on the boy without making any sound."

"The first we heard was the other kids screaming," added Condor. "Everyone came running. Almost everyone." His eyes went to Fat Bear who was standing a bit apart from the crowd.

"We tried to make the lion leave," Spruce Tree went on. "Yelled."

"Threw rocks," said Wolf Chaser. "Blackbird was brave." She gave the woman a look of approval. Maybe of admiration.

"Yeah, Blackbird and me got our spears and tried to chase it away from the body, but it dragged it away. We felt it best not to follow."

"And Dusk Light and Wolf Chaser backed us up," said Blackbird.

Condor nodded. "Followed our lead. I don't know where Fat Bear was. I saw no sign of him."

"Fat Bear was with me," spoke She Bear. Both Spruce Tree and Dusk Light immediately scowled, probably for completely different reasons. "Why not? She Bear has no one." She attempted a belligerent tone but ended up sounding defensive and maybe a little guilty.

"And you couldn't come help?" I asked, as calmly as I could. Best to turn this exchange back to the lion and poor little Moss.

Fat Bear felt it time to bluster and deflect. "Weren't you the one on guard here, Condor? I'm not responsible for what happened!"

"Just as you weren't responsible for what happened to Jad," replied Condor, his voice low but with an undercurrent of menace.

"I don't know what you're talking about," objected the big man, stepping back.

Whether Fat Bear had been negligent, whether he had been responsible for Jad's death, it was best this go no further. "One thing is certain," I stated. "We shall need to hunt this lion and kill it."

"And you're going to lead us?" Fat Bear's voice had at once become mocking, dismissive.

"With the approval of the tribe."

That I had, judging by the murmurs of the women. Even that of Spruce Tree. "Yes, Spear Thrower Bear Chaser Lynx. You will kill the lion." She turned to Fat Bear. "The fat one will go with you." She glared past him at She Bear for a second before turning away.

I do not think she would have minded Fat Bear being with the other woman had it been open. It was likely She Bear was not thinking about her, though, when she made her secret tryst, but the disapproval of her sister. Fat Bear, of course, would have had sex with any woman who would have him and think nothing of it.

"We should scout tomorrow," I decided. We might find what remained of the boy. We might learn where the lion liked to hole up. We might do many things.

\* \* \*

Black Bird spoke to me after our supper. It was quite dark outside. Fall was upon us.

"I have mentioned our suspicions about Jad's death to the women. They don't care." She spoke this with an air of detach-ment—a scientist reporting an interesting fact. "That is men's business, they say."

"Murder?"

"Fighting, anyway. These people do have their violent side, you know. They are human. And they expect the men to work things out among themselves."

That was a go-ahead of sorts, wasn't it? The women would not object if there was violence involving Fat Bear. I had no intention of initiating any but it was good to know.

Things had been tense during the meal. Spruce Tree had slid a little distance away from Fat Bear when he took his seat beside her. Not a repudiation but definitely a rebuke. Had Fat Bear accepted it as such, things might have settled down.

Instead, he attempted to assert himself. "Get over here woman," he growled.

She ignored him, her face expressionless. That there was much going on inside Spruce Tree I had no doubt.

He hesitated, uncertain, and then said, "There are other women here." His eyes went to She Bear.

197

"And other men," she immediately replied.

Dusk Light laughed at that. Fat Bear took a step forward but Condor was on his feet at once, flint blade in his hand.

She Bear looked at Condor for a moment, got up and went to sit beside him. Her sister gave a blink of approval. She might have even been urging this.

But it took Condor by surprise. He considered She Bear for few seconds, shrugged, and sat down.

"And don't look at me," came Blackbird's voice from somewhere behind me. That, perhaps, was an unnecessary taunt but she surely hated the man more than any of us.

Fat Bear turned our direction, only glancing at Blackbird but then staring at me. "I suppose you plan to hook up with Lynx," he spat out. "I know you two have been trying to undermine me here."

I could only laugh.

Fat Bear glared but said no more, settling down to resume his meal.

"You will have to kill him," Wolf Chaser whispered to me.

"I hope not," I whispered back. But I knew it might happen.

## 28.

IT WAS CONDOR WHO said, "Fat Bear is entirely likely to be friendly to us today, as if none of what happened matters. He'll see it as just another give and take with his rivals."

"But he would still be entirely willing to murder one of us if it seemed the right move," I said.

"I doubt he planned to murder Jad. He just saw an opportunity and took it without thinking. That's the man's way."

"He's impulsive," said Blackbird.

I nodded an agreement. "He does know he needs us though. Some of us." I regarded Condor for a moment. "You probably the least."

"And he sees me as his chief rival. I think the old Bear still believes he can bully you into submission. You, too," he added, inclining his head toward Blackbird.

"Ha! I'll not be joining his harem. Nor yours, you should know."

"So there's hope for Raven and me?"

She laughed, taking it in the spirit I asked it. "Oh, no, I'm just waiting for Spear Maker to grow up a little more."

The three of us were scouting for the lion. Vultures had already led us to the remains of little Moss. There had been no reason to drive them from their meal. Not much had remained. It was a good starting place to attempt to track the big cat.

And it was a good opportunity to speak, to make plans. Raven and Spear Maker and, yes, even Fat Bear could keep an eye on the tribe—not that the women couldn't keep an eye out themselves and use a spear if need be. It was understood they must be cautious.

The spoor we followed led south, toward where we had first spied the lion. He must be more comfortable in his familiar territory. He might have a den, a cave, somewhere. He was a cave lion, after all. We lost his tracks among the rocks.

"He may come back or he may not," was all I could report on our return to the cave, "but I would suspect he will, having killed once. All the men should go and try to rout him out soon. We won't be safe until the lion is dead."

"Yes," agreed Spruce Tree. "Now we gather acorns."

* * *

And gathering acorns was the sensible thing to do. They were mature and ready and could not be passed up as a food source. The tribe had not done that last year. There had been no men to accompany an expedition to the wood.

All the tribe went, of course, down the little river to where the oaks grew. It was not a large forest by any means but worth the journey. Condor accompanied us only as far as the pond. "I'm more useful catching fish than picking up fallen acorns," he had argued.

"But that means one less guard," I told him.

"Let Condor fish," said Spruce Tree, and that was the end of it. All the other women seemed to agree. Maybe they had a hankering for trout.

So we spent the better part of a day under the trees picking up acorns. We could have picked up more but we wouldn't have been able to carry them back. As it was, we were burdened with large leather bags full of them. They might not taste like much but they would be a further bulwark against starvation in the coming season.

The walnuts I had noted before were not ready. Maybe we could return for them. Weren't the nuts useful for tanning hides? This tribe seemed to have no idea of that. We would soon be gathering hazelnuts too.

Here and there, leaves were changing. Not so many yet. Did these Neanderthals appreciate their beauty? Did they appreciate their warning of the cold to come?

Fat Bear was as amiable as could be, seeming to have no rancor toward anyone. I can not say he worked particularly hard, however, spending more time chatting and attempting to charm the women. I could see they were already warming to him again. But I doubted he could get She Bear away from Condor!

It was Raven who fell in beside me as we started the trek home. He remained silent for some time. "I've tried to, um, stay out the way," he said at last. "Not take sides."

"You'd rather be off roaming on your own," I said.

"Exactly."

Nothing more, so I said, "I understand that. I've been a lone wanderer at times myself." As a kid. After my divorce. There had been times I needed to be alone, to explore both the wilderness and myself.

"Last Star tells me you think Fat Bear murdered Jad."

That was bound to get to him at last. "We think it is possible. Likely, even."

"I guess I can believe it. I didn't want to see how he was for a long time. You would think I'd be more knowledgeable about character, wouldn't you?" A moment's hesitation, a deep breath. "He's good at spinning things. I think maybe I was a little jealous of you and he sensed it. Played on it."

"Of me?"

"Yeah. Your competence." He snickered. "Your smugness."

I wasn't going to argue that one. I knew there was some validity to it. "You know I've tried to keep out of things too," I said. "It can't always be done."

He looked to the hills around us. We had left the woods and were in open country. "Unless I just went off by myself. I have a desire to explore this world. Not in winter though."

"I would think not." I wondered how soon the first snow would fall. Too soon, no doubt. "There's Condor."

"Egg in a Nest Condor Fish Catcher!" exclaimed Dusk Light, spying the string of char and trout he hoisted.

"Fish Catcher, eh? I could live with that name," he said, falling in with us. "Looks like it's been a good day for the hunting and the gathering."

"That it has," I agreed. "And we need more good days."

\* \* \*

Our torches were made of twigs, reeds, grasses twisted together. They needn't last long; we had left the cave in darkness so we could reach our destination before dawn. That was the cliff of the bees. Frost lay silver-white on the heather and sedge, and our breath clouded the air before us.

Spear Maker and Raven were with me. So were Wolf Chaser and Blackbird. We carried many ropes. I intended to be the one lowered to the nest but had informed no one of this. Now, by the light of the rising sun, I laid out my plan. "The men will lower me from the top," I announced, "and I will throw the combs down to the women." I was probably being too competent and smug but Raven made no remark.

"We want to hang on the ropes too!" proclaimed Wolf Chaser.

"Yeah," added Blackbird.

"We'll see. I'm definitely going first." They knew not to argue with me on that.

I did not feel competent. In fact, I had no idea what I was doing. I could only hope the cold would keep the bees from swarming me. I could be wrong. I could be stung badly. All the more reason to go first. Down I was lowered on two stout lines, holding a stick and a bag made from the stomach of the last deer we had taken. Despite the cold, I left my hide cape above, wearing only a loincloth.

The two women descended to the base of the cliff, going roundabout on the grassy slopes. They, too, had bags. Maybe more than needed but there was no telling how much honey might be back inside that crevice. It ran at least ten or maybe twelve feet in length, and perhaps two at its widest point. Depth? I'd find out.

A long trail of dried honey ran from the bottom of the crack to the ground below. It might have been dripping slowly down for years or centuries. I came even with the top end. "Hold!"

No bees were moving, much less flying. That was to the good. I somewhat gingerly probed with my stick. It came out sticky with honey. I sampled a finger's worth. Surprisingly mild flavor. Time to dig. In I shoved the stick again and pried out a chunk of comb. There were bees with it, too sluggish to cause trouble. I tossed it down.

"Lower!" And so I went down the face of the cliff. Where honey oozed out, I tried to direct it into my bag. Where combs could be pulled or pushed from the rock, they were. I was covered with honey. A bear would probably think me the most wonderful of treats.

"Make sure you remove the bees!" I called down. It wouldn't do to have them waking up inside their bags.

"They're all full!" Blackbird called up to me. I hadn't even gone halfway down. There would be plenty enough honey left for another day. Or for the bees. We didn't want to destroy their hive, after all. It was a renewable resource, something that could be tapped year after year.

Year after year. I should keep my mind on the present and not make long-term plans. Surviving this winter was what mattered now. The honey would help. I was hoisted back to the clifftop, slowly. I noted a dark band in the white limestone but hadn't the time to think of it right then.

"You're quite a mess," observed Raven. Spear Maker just

reached out and plucked a bee that was stuck to me. He looked it over, pulled the stinger out, and popped it into his mouth.

"Too fuzzy," he complained, after swallowing it down.

"And I'm too sticky. Let's get down to the girls."

That took a couple minutes. When we got there I asked Wolf Chaser if she still wanted to hang on a rope.

She looked up the face of the precipice. "We have enough honey," she decided.

That we did. I went to the damp seepage at the base of the cliff and cleaned as much of it off myself as I could, rubbing and rolling. I'd have to get in the stream and finish when we returned home. No matter how cold it was.

*  *  *

It had been a good day, I thought, as night fell. Things had gone well at the cave. No confrontations had arisen. The honey had been well received. Things looked good for our future, for the coming winter. We would continue to prepare and weather whatever was to come.

I was happy. Wolf Chaser lay beside me, her slow steady breathing telling me she had already fallen into sleep. It was good to feel her warm body against mine. Did I need more?

As I settled down to a peaceful and satisfied sleep, I heard the lion cough in the dark cold night.

# 29.

ALL THE MEN OF the tribe—that included Spear Maker—went on the hunt. Spruce Tree and I warned everyone to remain close to the cave while we were gone. And to remain vigilant.

South we went, seeking the lion in his lair. We might or might not be able to locate the beast. It was better than waiting for him to show up again, perhaps to take another of the tribe.

"After we kill the lion we will kill the wolves," stated Spear Maker, with far more assurance than any of the rest of us felt. Two hours we walked, slowly, taking our time, paralleling our little stream as it diminished and turned more easterly.

"If nothing else comes of this," I said, "we can at least cut some more spruce up here."

"Too early for a Christmas tree," was Condor Fish Catcher's response. More of the tribe were calling him Fish Catcher now and I felt he rather liked it.

Fat Bear's question was more to the point. "Couldn't we bait it somehow? Stake out an animal or some meat or something?"

"Are you volunteering?" asked Fish Catcher. Fat Bear said no more, dismissing the remark with a laugh.

It hadn't been a bad suggestion. But if we caught anything big enough to entice our neighborhood lion, we would probably choose to eat it ourselves. We kept our eyes open—those of us who knew what to look for. Tracks, or a kill, maybe. I scanned the skies for vultures from time to time, though, of course, there were other creatures that made kills. The wolves. Hyenas, if any were in the vicinity. I had seen no sign in the time we had been here but the women assured us they existed in the area.

Or even a bear. According to Blackbird, the cave bear was largely a vegetarian. That was reassuring. It did not mean, however, they wouldn't kill if the opportunity presented itself. The idea of taking a bear or two to add to our stores was still present in my mind. But today, the lion was our quarry.

We were equipped as well as we might be. That it might prove inadequate was certainly on my mind, and probably those of the others. Maybe not Spear Maker. Each carried two or three spears and, as usual, a hand ax. Raven had gone a step further and lashed a flint blade to a handle. Spear Maker greatly admired the result. I fully expected him to put together his own hafted ax when we returned home.

I myself was thinking more along the lines of a handle for a knife. Maybe bone. "The lion," came Spear Maker's sudden hoarse whisper, bringing me out of my tool-making reverie. I looked about in sudden alarm before realizing he pointed to tracks in the sand.

Large tracks. I was reminded again just what a formidable creature we hunted. "Fresh," I commented.

"Isn't it likely to be holed up for the day?" asked Raven. "It was hunting last night, I would assume."

"If he caught anything," I said. I wasn't sure I would want to face a hungry lion. A full, sleepy one would be preferable, but harder to draw out. I gave the tracks another look. "He was headed back the way we came. Maybe going down to get a drink."

"Or stalking us," Fish Catcher had to add.

"Or headed toward the cave. Let's follow the spoor." As we started off, I added, "We'll want to keep close to the rocks. We don't want to come face to face with it in the open."

A moment later, as we skirted a steep, rocky slope, we did come face to face with the lion. It was not too close, which was fortunate. Fifty yards? I don't know. Maybe more. I do know it rushed us at once across the open, slightly upward-sloping ground, and the number of yards separating us quickly diminished.

Spear Maker launched his projectile first. I threw my spear a second or two later, though neither of us had a good angle. The others? I'm not sure why but I am sure no one else attempted to attack. My eyes were on the massive beast which had suddenly veered in its charge and then stopped, seemingly baffled, and licked at a spot on his flank. One of us must have grazed the lion. That would not stop him.

"Into the rocks!" I called, though I had my second spear at the ready. I think my companions might have already been climbing. The steepness would slow the lion down when he again charged. I thought it likely he would. We could use our spears here, repel him, maybe even try to kill him. I was amazed that I thought of any of that in those few seconds as I climbed. I did not panic. My mind felt clear, almost as if time slowed down.

I remember once as a kid how I slipped on a wet forest slope covered with fallen leaves and could not stop myself as I slid toward a low cliff. I was just as lucid, and completely prepared to make as good a landing as I could when I went over the edge. Fortunately, I suffered no worse than a sprained ankle that day, and some scratches from falling among brambles!

I can't speak as to the condition of my comrades. The lion roared loudly, perhaps in rage over his minor hurt, perhaps unhappy that we seemed to be escaping, and came on again, more cautiously now. I thought I was in as good a spot to defend against him as any. I could only hope the others had positioned themselves as well—and near me. Spear Maker, at least, had the sense to do that. I could see him from the corner of my eye. He had his spear ready, a little to my left.

To my right I watched Fat Bear scrambling to the top of a low outcropping. A good spot. Condor was already there. Was he offering his erstwhile friend and current enemy a hand up?

No. Suddenly the hand shot out and I could see the glitter of the flint blade. Fat Bear fell backward and rolled down the slope. In a moment the lion was upon him. All this happened in silence.

I didn't think Spear Maker had seen it happen. His eyes had been on the lion. Where was Raven? Ah, over there. He might not have had a good view of events either. The beast dragged Fat Bear's body a short distance and settled down to feed. I waved the others to me.

"This is the best opportunity we'll have to kill it," I whispered to them. "It is likely to ignore us if we approach."

"All of us with spears!" spoke Spear Maker. "All at once!"

Yeah, that was pretty much what I had in mind. But Raven said, "There are some pretty big rocks up here. Maybe we could lever one down on it."

"Or an whole avalanche," said Fish Catcher.

It might be worth a try. But no— "We'll try spears first," I decided. "Those who are willing."

To their credit, both were. And of course Spear Maker had been ready all along and chafed to get at it. "Stay where you can bolt back into the rocks if you need to," I warned. "And watch out for each other. Be ready to protect anyone the lion charges."

We slowly made our way down and inched closer to the feeding cat. It eyed us occasionally and let out a low growl but I do not think it considered us an actual threat. Maybe he saw us as no different from the scavengers waiting to share the remains of his meal. Eventually, we would get too close and he would react.

Whether he would choose to attack or drag the body further away, I didn't know. Either way, he might rise and present a target. We had best strike quickly—and be prepared to run!

The lion's tail lashed back and forth. He was getting nervous. "Be ready," I ordered. I hoped I said it loud enough. We were spread out a little but keeping as close to the rocks as possible. It would not be at all wise to get on the other side of the beast. We were in good range. Wait—

He rose, snarling, but facing us head on. It was Spear Maker who threw a small rock, glancing off the right flank of the lion, which turned that way with a snarl, snapping with fearsome jaws. At once, spears flew. He sprang toward us—and sprang no further, collapsing. With my third spear in hand, which was nothing more than a sharpened stick, I moved in. Spear Maker got there before me and drove his weapon into its side; the others followed.

"Hold," I said, holding up a hand. "No sense in ruining the skin." The lion was certainly dead. As was his victim.

Euclid Ball's death had been swift and sudden. I don't know if the knife did much damage but when the lion hit him it was over almost at once. Had Condor Fish Catcher planned something like this or did he also choose to take advantage of an opportunity? I did not know. Nor would I ask or even mention it. It was over.

Maybe in time I would have found it necessary to do something of the same sort.

\* \* \*

"It was Raven's spear that drove into the lion's heart," I told the tribe, as they gathered around us. "I name him Lion Killer."

I hoped the name would stick. The lion skin was handed over to the women. We had not brought any of its meat, over Spear Maker's objections. We did carry home what remained of Fat Bear. He would receive an honorable sky burial, the same as Jad. What mattered it if one had killed the other?

What mattered it if Fish Catcher had killed him? We had winter to face. That did matter. I decided to say nothing of what had happened to anyone. No, not even to Blackbird. I could not prevent Fish Catcher from saying something if he wished. "Fat Bear slipped climbing to escape the lion," was the official tale I told the tribe that night. It is to be noted there was little wailing for him. Not even from Spruce Tree.

In the darkness after our evening meal, as a small fire flickered in the gloom and many sought their sleeping places, Condor Fish Catcher came to where I sat by the entry. I had chosen to take sentry duty this evening. I knew I would not sleep if I lay down now.

He sat beside me a few minutes, wordless. Then he said, "I have no desire to be the boss here, Lynx. I would leave it to someone with more vigor left in him. Preferably you. Raven's bright but not a leader."

"You mean Lion Killer," I said.

He snorted. "It took more than one spear to kill that lion."

"As it takes more than one to lead this tribe."

# Part III.
# That Cold Time

## 30.

WOLF CHASER WAS THE first of the women to be obviously pregnant. There was no question as to who was the father. That would not be so if any of the others were with child.

"You must take Spruce Tree as your woman," she told me. "I do not mind."

"Not right away," I had responded. I recognized the wisdom of what she urged.

"No, not right away."

But in time, I did sit down by Spruce Tree and she accepted me. Yes, we had sex. And yes, the tribe saw me as their leader. In an informal sense. The idea of a 'chief' was not one that existed for them. I was the first among the men, as Spruce Tree was among the women.

Through September—what I assumed to be September—we gathered and hunted, as before. We harvested hazelnuts and walnuts. We gathered more acorns. I led the men on hunts and we got better at it. The fact that it was mating season for the deer, and the bucks became less cautious might have helped us there! It was perhaps as well that Fat Bear was gone. He had consumed more calories than he contributed. We fell into a peaceful routine and October came and the first snows.

With them came the reindeer. Already had I seen the water-fowl passing through, on their way to warmer climes. Africa, perhaps, where men like myself—more or less—lived. It might be a better life, a less demanding life, there.

But I could not go, nor would I if I could. "We must go to the lake to hunt," I announced. "Now, or it will be too late." I had once thought of journeying over the hills to the 'great stream,' the proto-Tiber, but I knew the impracticality of that. Even attempting to take the tribe to our lake and camp a few days could bring all sorts of unknown dangers. What if a blizzard came unexpectedly? What if the footprint we saw was the sign of an unfriendly tribe in the area?

So the tribe walked eastward. Not all of us; Wolf Chaser and She Bear we left to mind the cave and watch after the youngest children. Best neither the little ones nor pregnant women join our march.

Though I found later that more than one of the women on our march was pregnant. In fact, all of them were. Even Blackbird. We can get into all that later.

* * *

"I miss Moss," said Nut Grass, traipsing along at my side. I seemed to be his adopted father figure. And Moss had been his brother, not that blood relationship meant much. All these kids were like one family.

"He is gone from our cave," I said, "but he lives now in a land far away." I felt I did no wrong it telling him this. There was another Moss. Many Mosses, perhaps, in other timelines. In some he surely survived.

"Far away," he repeated. "Is my mother there?"

Why not? "He is with her."

I think the boy sniffled but he walked on resolutely.

We all walked on. There was no reason to stop. Some of us gnawed on dried meat as we went. With the scarcity of fuel, fresh roasted meat was not frequently on the menu at the cave; much of what we ate had been dried. It was, strictly, raw but curing the meat did in a sense cook it. Most of what we took on this expedition—or hoped to take—would also end up being dried but I hoped for at least one feast.

Firewood. That was another thing we needed to plan for before the bitter cold came. There would not be much available but we could cut trees now in the vicinity of the cave—maybe even as far away as the little piece of forest downstream—and leave them lying, to be gathered later when dried a bit. There would be the gathering of reindeer dung of course. We should be able to find some from the aurochs, too, but it wouldn't be practical to carry it all the way home from the lake. I hoped to use it as fuel while we were there.

"We should name the lake," I suddenly announced. I don't think any of the Neanderthals knew what I meant. They didn't name landmarks, other than by description. To them, this was the lake beyond the hills where the sun rose. Or the lake where the aurochs drink, as I heard Spear Maker refer to it more than once.

"I vote for Arnold," said Blackbird. "All in favor?"

Both Fish Catcher and Raven Lion Killer raised their hands. Some of the others did too, but I am sure they had no idea why.

"As Great Chief, I veto this," I proclaimed, "and hereby name it Lake Jad."

There were only sober nods of agreement. I had not expected any objections. Jad had been there when first we spied it shimmering in the distance.

In a generation no one would know why it was named so. If the name was still used. That did not matter; we would use it now. It was nearing noon when we crossed the last ridge and looked down on Lake Jad. The first thing to catch my eye was the herd of mammoths.

A small herd, to be sure, but even a small herd was a lot of meat. One mammoth was a lot of meat. I hadn't the slightest hope of taking one. Not on this open land. In the hills it might be feasible, if one knew narrow places through which they traveled. There were other herds here too. More reindeer than the few who had trickled through our valley so far. I wondered if they might winter around here.

We would find out, I supposed. I had no idea how mobile we could be during the coldest months. Could we make our way here to hunt? The lake would surely be frozen, the waterfowl gone, but I suspected the aurochs wintered over, as do American bison.

Excited chatter began to rise from the women and children, first hushed, almost whispered, but growing louder. They had never traveled here before; their vanished menfolk might have but they hadn't let the women in on their secrets. "We will camp there," I announced, pointing toward the west end of the water. This had been discussed with the others before we began. There was higher land there and rocky places where we could shelter ourselves—some—if need be.

Also the aurochs would be less likely to trample on us.

\* \* \*

"It is impressive," admitted Blackbird. "It's too bad there is no cave close to here."

"I would think our valley is better sheltered from the winter weather," I replied. "I can imagine the polar winds blowing across this open land." We sat on a rock outcropping and surveyed the wide valley, lying green before us, the lake shimmering gold as the sun set. There were the aurochs, coming down to the water. The mammoths too. How many? A half-dozen? And a couple of them juveniles.

"I wonder when the mammoths breed," I said.

"Summer and early fall, we believe. They would have a long gestation, like a year and a half or more, so that works out for giving birth in spring."

"I should have known you would have that sort of info at your fingertips." I regarded the little herd for a moment. "So we don't have to worry about belligerent, horny males right now."

"Only you and Fish Catcher!" There came a long pause before she continued in a more serious, more subdued voice. "Fish Catcher told me how Yukey met his end and the part he played in it." She glanced at me from the corner of her eye before gazing

217

out over the valley bowl again. "And he says you saw what went down. He doesn't know about the others."

"I think they didn't. If they did, they'd just as soon not talk about it. Me too."

She nodded. "I understand that. He doesn't plan to mention it to anyone else."

"But he thought you should know." I wasn't sure if I was stating that or asking a question. A bit of both, I guess.

"Yeah. I suspect none of the women would mind the least if the truth were known. Ha, I doubt it would hurt Fish Catcher's reputation, either."

In the distance, a wolf howled. Another voice rose to join it. Our local pack or another? Maybe some followed the reindeer south. We would have to be watchful. As ever. Day faded, but a full moon hung in the eastern sky—the Harvest Moon, I thought it would be, not the Hunter's Moon. Either way, it had been one of the reasons I chose to make the trip at this time. I felt safer with that full moon lighting the evenings.

There would be no fire tonight, not even a small one, though we carried coals to start one. The folk, this tribe, could create fire if necessary but it was a nuisance to need bother. We ate a cold meal and wrapped ourselves in hides, settling down on new grass beds. Grass, at least, was in ready supply here. I chose to sit the first shift as sentry.

A mammoth trumpeted somewhere out there in that moonlit valley. The lake lay placid, silver. I had seen geese descend to its shelter as the day waned. Blackbird was right; this would be a good place to live if there were a suitable cave near enough.

What did I need of a cave? I knew how to build a cabin, or at least some sort of dugout house that could be set into these hills. Were I on my own.

But I was not. This tribe, this world, was not ready for houses. I turned to look them over, dark forms slumbering in a little hollow spot we had chosen among the rocks, before gazing again out over the valley below us. Tomorrow, we would hunt. That was what was needed.

# 31.

BLACKBIRD HAD TAKEN TO painting a wavy line on her arm with the dark ocher clay, in emulation of the other women's ritual scarring. She carried the pigment with her in a little pouch, a bladder or stomach from some small animal. Spying it this morning led to sudden inspiration. I'd call it inspiration, anyway. "I need one of those," I announced.

"Are you going to start painting yourself?" she asked.

"Nope. I meant the pouch. You'll see what I have in mind. Hmm, I do wonder if we could find some other colors than that raw sienna." I thought on that only a moment. "We'll have to keep an eye open." It did not seem overly important. We needed to keep our eyes open for other resources too. Especially stone for the making of tools.

"Black can come from ashes. And that chalky limestone we find everywhere could probably provide a decent white pigment," Blackbird said. "Grind it fine and mix it with a tad of fat."

"Aren't deposits of flint found in that kind of rock? Or in marble or something, right?"

"I believe so. I do know marble cutters sometimes complain about hitting it."

That was what I had heard too. It wasn't much to go on, but I remembered the darker rock in the cliff of the bee hive. That I should investigate. "We could go up to Carrara and get all the best marble long before anyone else knows about it," I said.

"And build ourselves palaces?"

"Oh, I want an heroic statue of myself."

"If anyone here knew how to make one, you'd probably have it. What are you staring at?" I was gazing past her, into the misty distance below us.

"There." I pointed.

There was a quick drawing in of her breath. "A human." She scanned the valley. "I only see the one."

It would have been easy enough to miss others, were they there. "I wonder if he's seen us."

Blackbird shrugged. "We'll be hard to miss the next few days. If he is alone, it will be up to him to approach us."

That was so. "We might as well get busy then."

\* \* \*

Busy indeed. I had a long list of chores for us. In my head, of course. Hmm, I could probably improvise a way of writing things down, couldn't I? Another thing to think upon through the winter. No time now!

"We should have started earlier for the waterfowl," I announced to the camp. "Before dawn." To be sure, I did not say 'waterfowl,' as they had no such word. I've explained that before, I think.

Spruce Tree pointed toward the prairie lying along the north side of Lake Jad. "We will gather there," she said. No one voiced opposition to the plan. Certainly not me.

"You'll want to set your snares," I said to Lion Killer.

"Many, many rabbits," Spear Maker added to this. Yeah, we knew.

"There might be a warren somewhere," I went on. "Or more

than one. We'll have to keep an eye out." We'd be keeping an eye out for many things, this first day. Our stranger included.

Nut Grass was one of the children with us; Acorn was about the same age but had been left behind to help She Bear and Wolf Chaser. Today, Nut Grass accompanied the women. We impressed on him that he was the man in charge. And to do what he was told.

Blackbird went with the women too, though I am sure she would rather have been with us. Little Rabbit did tag along with the men; she was Lion Killer's assistant, carrying as many snares as her arms could hold. Those had improved somewhat in design since our first days with the tribe. Lion Killer had absorbed considerable knowledge of the materials available to the Neanderthals, the sinews and fibers, the different sorts of wood, to refine the traps.

"Those snares might well be the most valuable technology we have brought to this tribe," I observed, to no one in particular.

"Don't forget your spear thrower," replied Lion Killer. "Let's put one here. I hope we remember where we set them all."

I trusted the Neanderthals to do that. I knew I wouldn't, though I looked about at landmarks in an attempt to fix the location in my memory. There were signs of a pathway; some creature or another must pass this way. We continued toward the lake. Lake Jad. I could see winged forms appear and disappear in the mists blanketing the surface and its marshy margins.

"Snow geese, maybe?" I conjectured. "Something like them. I don't know what sort of waterfowl lived here in the past."

"You mean in the present," Fish Catcher reminded me.

Thin ice lay along the shoreline when we reached it, extending no more than a couple feet into the water. I'd had thoughts of wading in. I thought differently now. "It's going to be too cold to get into the lake," I said. "I had been considering going in after the ducks."

Fish Catcher considered this as well. "Our young companions might handle it better. If we try wading into there we'll end up with hypothermia." He gazed across the fog-shrouded lake. "I'd been thinking of trying to fish."

"Then we need a boat," stated Lion Killer.

Fish Catcher didn't hide his skepticism toward this idea. "Where would we get the wood?"

"A hide boat. We could use willow or hazel wands for the framing of it."

"Or even bones," I added. "I don't think we could make one now but we should definitely have a boat next time we visit."

Our two Neanderthals had no idea what we were talking about, but waited stolidly for us to finish. They had learned our quirks and that it was best to ignore them.

"Lake Jad will undoubtedly freeze over soon," said Fish Catcher. "I could try ice fishing."

This seemed doubtful to me. "It would be a difficult journey in winter."

Lion Killer looked to the expanse of tall reeds, motionless on this still morning, and back to us, with a faint smile. "We could even make a reed boat right now. More like a raft, maybe."

Fish Catcher and I looked at each other. "Good idea," he said. "The kid's not as dumb as he looks."

I nodded. "There's a lot can be done with reeds." My thoughts went at once to the making of a reed house. I remembered some Native Americans made lodges from mats woven of cattails, lodges they inhabited comfortably through harsh winters. Maybe we could do something similar.

But not on this day! Nor on this journey. It was something for the future, for spring, maybe. If we made it to spring. "What sort of reeds these might be I have no idea, but there are certainly plenty of them. Let's try cutting some when the sun is higher."

"After I set the rest of the snares," said Lion Killer, "and all I know is they're not papyrus." We set off again.

\* \* \*

There was more reconnoitering than hunting that day, watching and learning. The reindeer most took our attention, for they were numerous, and large enough to provide plenty of meat. It was a pleasant day, warmed by a light breeze from the south-west, with clouds scudding across the sun through the morning.

By afternoon, the sun was hidden, those clouds looming low over the broad valley. Rain came and went, light. By the lakeside we constructed our boat, wading in with our hand axes to hack among the reed beds, standing higher than us, and binding the stalks into bundles. For this, we used both the reeds themselves and slender willow branches we cut nearby.

"It looks more like a pointy raft than a boat," commented Fish Catcher.

"As long as it floats, I don't care," I told him. I gave it a long looking over. "Floats one of us," I added. "I don't think it would take two." Not enough to keep them dry, anyway.

"You're the lightest," said Lion Killer. The implication was that I should be test pilot.

"Not counting Rabbit. Okay, let's get it into the water."

Rabbit, of course, was baffled by our construction. "Is it a bed?" she had whispered to Spear Maker.

He wasn't sure but had an inkling of its true purpose. "They will hide behind it to sneak up on ducks," he decided.

We slid it into the shallows and I climbed into—or onto, more properly—the craft. Water did come through the bundled reeds, to be sure, but they floated me higher than I had expected. Higher than I had hoped, even. I poled around a little with the shaft of my spear.

"I'll need to make a paddle," I called. Hmm, how? I'd have think on that. The bottom was soft, making it hard to plant my pole. I started to attempt to turn the ungainly raft about and then laughed. All I had to do was turn myself around!

I poled back to the shore and we pulled it up onto solid ground. "Enough for the maiden voyage. Before dawn, we'll get down here and try to sneak up on the ducks, as Spear Maker has suggested." I looked up. "We have time to hunt before returning."

Hunt we did and managed to surprise a reindeer just as dusk was falling. I was pleased to see three of our spears strike the creature. Spear Maker's and Lion Killer's and mine, that is; Fish Catcher did not attempt a cast. That was just as well.

We carried the carcass, not bothering with any butchery as night was near, back to the camp. A small fire burned there, fed from a pile of aurochs chips. A surprising amount of dried dung had been gathered.

Also surprising was that they had gathered a young Neanderthal man.

# 32.

I AWOKE TO A dusting of snow. Spruce Tree lay beside me.

Spear Maker was poking at me. "We go," he insisted.

It was comfortable under the fur, with my woman's warm body against my own. I did not want to get up.

I sighed and slid from beneath the skins. I'd told the boy to wake me before dawn, after all. It was going to be only we two, down to the lake and my boat. Lion Killer would stir in an hour or two, come down to check his snares. With a stranger in our midst, I preferred he and Fish Catcher be in camp.

Not that the kid seemed any sort of threat. He was certainly more apprehensive than the women who had brought him back.

"I'm coming too," spoke a voice from the darkness. The little fire smoldered but cast no light. The stars glimmered, however, and a full moon, setting now, scattered silver across the lake.

I only grunted an acknowledgment. Blackbird fell in beside us as we descended from the rocks. I figured she wanted to talk. Or maybe she was curious. We had talked up the reed boat a bit.

The sound of waterfowl drifted up to us, distant, faint. The birds would be launching soon, continuing their journey south, following the sun to Africa. It was far too late to for us to make that journey.

"What do you make of Duck Hunter?" she asked. That was the name the women had bestowed on our newcomer, for he had been carrying a duck when he approached them. What he called himself no one could say. Except Duck Hunter himself, and he spoke a dialect none understood. Blackbird had managed to puzzle out a few words but they had mostly communicated with the boy through signs.

Yes, boy. Still a teen, for sure. Why he was wandering alone he might be able to tell us, in time. There would be time. Winter is long.

"I think he was fortunate to find us. He would not have survived the winter alone."

"He was very uncertain about revealing himself. I don't think he would have if men were there." She stifled a giggle. "Nut Grass became very protective."

As had Spear Maker as soon as we had arrived at the camp. He practically bristled at the intruder. Now he marched stolidly forward, pretending he wasn't listening. "I think Spear Maker sees him as a rival for your hand," I whispered to Blackbird.

"Maybe he will be," she whispered back. That subject I felt it best not to pursue.

Our reed raft rested where we had left it. "It could probably carry two," I said.

Spear Maker shook his head. He'd learned that gesture from us but it seemed to come natural to him now. "I will hunt along the edge of the water," he told us, his voice low. We all spoke in little more than whispers, though it might not have made any differ-ence. The calls of the fowl were subdued, ghostly, floating through the misty predawn. It was a morning that seemed to call for a certain reverence.

Not that it would get it from Blackbird. "You need a retriever," she said, as she assisted me in pushing the boat into the lake. There was less ice than the previous day.

"I have one, back in Tennessee," I informed her. "The other me might be playing with him right now. Um, or sixty thousand years from now."

"I don't suppose it would be practical to try taming a wolf. The consensus is that they sort of tamed themselves."

"Not the old wolf cubs carried home bit we learned about as kids?"

"Nah. The ancestral dogs adopted us, not the other way around. They took to hanging around humans."

I had put together a paddle of sorts, a piece of hide stretched over a forked branch. It might not be necessary if I stuck to the shallow water around the reed beds. I took up my spear to pole myself away from the shore and gave my companion a questioning look.

"I'll do like Spear Maker," she decided, and disappeared into the fog.

Slowly, cautiously, I made my way through the reeds, towering above me, dripping with condensation. At least it wasn't freezing. There was barely enough light for hunting. I couldn't catch any ducks if I couldn't see them!

For hunting them, I could depend on my spear. I didn't have the skills for throwing rocks or sticks. That I could leave to Spear Maker. Or maybe the new guy.

I also carried a rudimentary net. Fish Catcher said he was adept with a cast-net but we hadn't attempted anything that complicated. This was simply a web of twisted string, with some rock weights along its edges. I had practiced tossing it back at the cave and sometimes it landed properly and sometimes it didn't.

One thing was certain—the closer I could get to my target, the better.

Dark forms floated ahead of me, ducks or geese, resting before they took again to the sky. I cast. Three geese honked in alarm, enmeshed, thrashing. I pulled them in, rung their necks as they beat their heavy wings against me, and poled on.

It was going to be a good morning

\* \* \*

"How is polygamist life working out for you?" asked Fish Catcher.

"Not bad. It's easier when we can leave one wife at home, isn't it?"

He only nodded, seemingly distracted. Thinking of his life before, I surmised, and the two women who had shared it in Miami.

We had returned to the camp while the sun was still low in the sky, only peeking over the distant eastern hills, with a dozen waterfowl. It was a heavy load for the three of us. Now we returned to the lake. Fish Catcher, living up to his name, wanted to attempt fishing from the raft.

"My teeth aren't the best," he had confided to me. "One reason I'd rather eat fish. Easier to chew, easier on the dental work." He had frowned at a thought. "If my bridge broke I'd be in trouble. No way I could chew that dried meat."

"Dusk Light would have to pre-chew it for you," I'd told him. That was already done for some of the smaller children. I told myself to experiment with pounding meat to make it more tender. The idea of making some sort of pemmican returned. Another project. They were piling up.

He carried his rod now. "If the boat doesn't work out, I can fish from the shore. It should be best where one of the streams flows in." He looked out across Lake Jad. "But there may be some big ones out there in the depths."

"If there are depths," I said. "It could all be shallow." We might have time to find out.

Spear Maker and Lion Killer walked a little ahead of us, checking the snares. I hoped Lion Killer could remember where they all were set. He might have to go back and ask Rabbit.

"Spear Maker has become somewhat attached to Raven," I remarked.

Fish Catcher's eyes rested on the pair for a few seconds. "The boy resents me just a little, I think, for being with his mother. She says he had hopes his dad would come back."

Though, according to Spruce Tree, his father probably wasn't who he thought he was. "You're better with kids than Lion Killer or me," I said. "Little kids, I mean. Rabbit had no problem switching her affections to you."

He considered this. "True, I guess. They like you but you're not always so approachable, you know."

I did know.

"Are you happy, Ken?"

I could only shrug. "Beats me. I'm not sure I know what the word means." That was the truth, no matter how lame it might have sounded. "I guess maybe I'm content. That hasn't been true in a long time."

"You have purpose. I think that's what drives you. You need to accomplish things."

That could be true.

He went on. "For me, it was always money. The respect and the good life it brings. Not much wealth available here!"

I had to chuckle. "You have as much as anyone in the tribe."

"Yes. The tribe's prosperity is my prosperity, and that's good enough for me." For a moment, I thought that was all he had to say. "For Ball, it was all about power. He needed to dominate."

"He was a paranoid narcissist," I stated, probably with more authority than I should have.

"Psychology?" Fish Catcher sounded amused.

"I've learned a few things."

He accepted that without comment. "Okay. So not a psychopath? That's what I would have said but I don't know anything."

"No offense intended, but maybe you and I fit that one better. I know I have trouble, um, empathizing sometimes. Or forming strong attachments." I attempted a self-deprecating smile. "It undoubtedly helped make me successful."

"Hmm, yeah, I guess that could be true of me too. We're getting attached here though, aren't we?"

I only nodded. Yes, I had an attachment to the tribe, to Wolf

Chaser. And I would be a father. Still, it wouldn't be too hard for me to leave, would it? Relationships came and went. I could only be certain I would be staying through the winter. That assumed I survived it.

The fifth member of our group followed behind us. Duck Hunter had attached himself to us after some hesitation. I guess he thought he should be with the men when they went hunting. The young Neanderthal looked pretty well fed. He'd had this valley to himself for some time, so that wasn't surprising. He was dark compared to our tribe, and his beard was sparse. Spear Maker was already well on the way to having a heavier one.

Ha, Duck Hunter's whiskers looked nearly as thin as my own. I had a suspicion—as did Blackbird—that he'd had a dose of modern human genes injected into his lineage at some point. But he looked pretty much Neanderthal otherwise.

We figured he'd been isolated long enough we needn't worry about any cataclysmic disease ravaging our tribe. By 'we,' I mean we time travelers. Who might know how much immunity these people—and we four even more so—might have to new strains of something as simple as a cold virus? Diseases such as tuberculosis or herpes were a completely different matter. They could lurk and debilitate over years, destroying a tribe or even a race. That could have been one factor in the waning of the Neanderthals.

It was something over which we would have no control.

"Another rabbit!" crowed Lion Killer.

* * *

"There are depths out there," Fish Catcher reported, "but I

233

don't believe any large fish lurk in them. How would they get here?"

He had a point. Lake Jad did not connect to any other bodies of water. "We could always stock it," I suggested. I was not at all serious and he knew it. But why not?

The catch from paddling about a good part of the day consisted of a few bottom-dwellers and some eels. I doubted we'd come back for ice fishing. We who hunted did better. Three times, we had stalked herds of grazing reindeer across the rolling valley and three times we had killed, Spear Maker and I. Duck Hunter was astounded, I think. He knew nothing of the atlatl and had been prepared to rush upon the beasts, to thrust or throw his spear at close range.

He also pretended not to be interested in our spear throwers. I hoped it was pretense—were he truly disinterested in learning something new, he might prove a burden to us. But Duck Hunter did seem a good addition to the tribe, young, healthy. Someday, we might learn why he wandered alone.

In fact, he might have been searching for a tribe to join. One with women. That's always been a good reason for young men to roam.

# 33.

"THE NEW GUY IS making eyes at me."

"He's making them at all the woman," said Fish Catcher. I'd noticed that as well.

Blackbird went on. "I think he's figured out I'm unattached. He wouldn't try to poach one of your women." She turned her eyes toward the young man, squatting on the other side of the fire. "It might be best if I'm not the one to give him language lessons."

We had a bigger fire this evening, for there was an ample supply of dung—primarily aurochs, as the reindeer droppings were still fresh, for the most part—and some of the meat was roasting. Most was being dried to carry back to the cave. It would mean heavy loads for all of us but we needed all we could cure for survival through the winter. Even then, it might not be enough. I had no idea whether any hunting would be possible when it grew bitterly cold.

"Next year," I said, "I do intend to go over to the Tiber. Maybe in the spring."

"The whole tribe?"

I could only shrug. "I'll have to talk with Spruce Tree about that." I looked out over the lake and valley, growing dark. I could see a flock of ducks dropping toward the reeds, hear their faint calls. I would rise early again tomorrow and take some of them. "We'll come back here too."

"I've been thinking," began Fish Catcher. He paused, softly chuckled. "Well, no it was Lion Killer's idea. I shouldn't claim it as my own. Couldn't get away with that in this small a group!

Anyway, two or three of us could pack a load of the dried meat back to the cave right now and return the next day."

"You?" asked Blackbird.

"I'd seem a good choice. I'm not as good at hunting as the rest of you."

"And you didn't find much in the way of fish," I said.

"That's true. Maybe Lion Killer and me and a couple of the women could make the trip."

By a couple, he probably meant their women, Last Star and Dusk Light. "Sounds good. Why don't you prepare to take off first thing in the morning?"

He nodded, rose, and went to discuss it with his mate. They waved Lion Killer to them a minute or so later. "I believe Last Star thinks I have designs on Lion Killer," said Blackbird, so softly I barely heard her.

"As long as you remain without a mate, all the women will suspect you," I replied. "Maybe you should claim the new guy."

She made a bit of a face. I chose not to ask about it.

Blackbird sat a moment more before stating, almost as quietly as before, "I'm pregnant."

I gave her a long look. "Does Last Star have reason to worry about you and Lion Killer?" I asked at last.

"No, not Lion Killer. I wouldn't let myself get entangled with him. Or you. You'd take it too seriously. That's not a problem with Fish Catcher."

I had nothing to say about that either. But plenty to think.

* * *

"I should build pack-boards," I said. "With tump-lines for the forehead. It would be a better way to haul those heavy loads."

Certainly better than the clumsy, haphazard bags and nets they were carrying. "We'll try to be back by tomorrow sunset," promised Fish Catcher. "I'll kiss your wife for you."

"That had better be all you do." The four figures disappeared into the mists of dawn. In theory, they could get back today but there was no need. The meat they packed was truly only half-cured and would need more attention when it reached the cave.

"So." I turned to Spear Maker and Duck Hunter. "What do we hunt today? Aurochs? Mammoth?"

Spear Maker knew I was joking. Duck Hunter recognized the word for mammoth. "Mammoth! Mammoth!" He shook his spear. I had to laugh. The boy reminded me of nothing so much as an out-sized Nut Grass. I think Spear Maker must have snickered too.

Our newest tribe member reddened and gave him a shove. "Hey," I admonished. "None of that." He didn't understand my words but he knew what I meant. And he became belligerent.

That might have been because the other two adult males were gone. This was his chance to assert himself. To challenge authority. In front of the women, too! Or so I guessed. He dropped his spear and crouched, arms out in front of him.

"I think he wants to wrestle you, Lynx, old boy," called Blackbird.

"A test of male dominance? Oh, well." I put my own spear down. At least the kid didn't want to fight with weapons. I grinned at him and took one step in. That was enough to get the Neanderthal to lunge at me. A left jab caught him squarely on his big schnoz. Duck Hunter abruptly sat, blood spurting from his nose and running down his chest.

Though he was larger and undoubtedly stronger than me, Duck Hunter did not know how to fight. Who would have taught him? There were no schools of Neanderthal martial arts, after all.

Honestly, I felt a little bad about having to clock the kid. "Let's get him cleaned up," I said to the two women who had remained. Spruce Tree was staring, first at me, then at Duck Hunter, apparently unsure what to think of what had happened. Blackbird smirked.

But it was Rabbit who came forward with a handful of grass and tried to wipe the boy clean. She gave me a decidedly unfriendly look. "I won't hurt him again," I promised her. "Do you think you can help him down to the lake?"

Spear Maker and I assisted the subdued Duck Hunter to his feet and accompanied him to the water, without words. Rabbit sometimes ran ahead a little and would wait for us to catch up. If she had been peeved at me for hurting the boy, that had evaporated.

I hoped any animosity he might feel against me had done the same. There was no telling about such things. "Rabbit and I must check the snares," said Spear Maker, as Duck Hunter cleaned himself in the frigid water. Rabbit sat watching him.

"You'll set new ones?"

He nodded. The two young Neanderthals could do this quite as well as Lion Killer now. Spear Maker called to his assistant. She jumped up, bade a cheerful farewell to Duck Hunter—which he may or may not have understood—and ran after her brother. I went down to see how my would-be opponent fared.

He might have a lop-sided nose the rest of his life. I hadn't intended to hit him that hard but it was such an easy and open target. "Camp?" I asked, trying to sound friendly. He knew that word by now.

Duck Hunter looked at me a bit warily and blinked an affirmation. The women were busy about their work when we arrived. With the others gone, Spruce Tree and Blackbird were not going to stray from camp. Too many youngsters needed to be watched and there was plenty of meat yet to cut up and cure. We had brought back more waterfowl early that morning, too, before the expedition to the cave set out. Those needed to be dressed.

Nut Grass ran up to us and then pantomimed my punching, clumsily, comically. Duck Hunter laughed and then winced. The nose would be painful for a while.

Blackbird had ambled over. "That's promising," she said. "But the boy has a temper. We'll have to watch that."

"He doesn't seem to hold a grudge."

"He could be hiding it and secretly planning revenge." She didn't sound serious, nor was I likely to take it so. "What if he had managed to grapple with you?"

"I would have had to fight dirty."

"I'd bet you're good at that." When she saw I intended to make no comment, she added, "I'd bet Fish Catcher is too."

I suspected I couldn't begin to rival him. "None of these Nean-derthals are likely to have much skill in combat," I said.

"Ah, then I'd be safe picking a fight with Last Star."

I only smiled at the quip but she was probably right.

"When the kids get back I'll go out hunting with Duck Hunter and Spear Maker. We want as much meat as we can get." I turned to survey the broad bowl, the grass still green in places, the herds moving here and there across it. "We all should return home in three or four days."

"Home," repeated Blackbird. There was certainly meaning in the way she said the word but I couldn't tell you what it might have been.

* * *

Spruce Tree stirred beside me. "Someone cries," she whispered.

Leave it to a mother to hear crying in the middle of the night. She was right. I was fully awake now and could hear sobbing. One of the children?

We both sat up and pushed our cover back, despite the cold and our nakedness. It's better to doff personal clothing when you're together under the furs. "Duck Hunter." She nodded her head toward a figure sitting at the edge of the camp, looking out over the lake. His shoulders heaved now and again.

I threw on my poncho and rose. Was the boy lonely? Or just overwhelmed by all that had occurred these two days with us? I couldn't talk with him but I could at least sit by him. Duck Hunter should know he wasn't alone here.

He glanced at me and turned away again. His cheeks were

streaked with tears. I said nothing. Maybe a reassuring hand on the shoulder would have helped and maybe it wouldn't. I decided to wait for now. Spruce Tree settled down on his other side and put an arm around the boy. Almost at once, his head fell onto her shoulder and he began to bawl.

He'd only needed a mother, maybe.

# 34.

"I'M NOT IN ANY way ready to tackle an aurochs," I informed Spear Maker. "Maybe when the others come back." I had my doubts we should attempt it even then.

I held the stomach of a rabbit in my hands. It had been well cleaned, turned inside out and allowed to dry thoroughly. Now I was stuffing bits of grass into it. It stretched somewhat more than I had expected. "That looks full enough," I announced. Spear Maker looked at it curiously but made no comment. He wasn't about to admit he had no idea what I was doing. "Some string—" I tied it off. "And we have a Paleolithic ball. Catch!" I called, and tossed it at Rabbit.

To her credit, she did. I'd half-expected her to duck. Moreover, she threw it back though it went nowhere near me.

"Much better than throwing rocks," I said, retrieving my errant toy. "Nut Grass!" I chucked the ball in his direction. He grabbed with both hands and missed with both, pouncing on it after it bounced off his chest. The boy threw it to Rabbit, grinning broadly.

"You guys play with that while we're hunting. Maybe I'll make some more of them. Ready to go?" I asked my pair of fellow hunters.

In answer, they set off, side by side, toward the basin of Lake Jad. Duck Hunter seemed to feel good enough this morning. His face, however, was a mess. I felt a little guilty about it. Purple and swollen it was, and he probably couldn't see too well with his right eye.

Weren't frequent injuries part of Neanderthal life? I'd read that they got busted up a lot. Their up-close hunting methods surely had something to do with that, especially if they tackled large game.

We'd do best to stick to the reindeer. I wasn't built to take a lot of damage. Even more reindeer seemed to be streaming into the valley from the north. I hadn't seen many move on but they must, eventually. It would not be any better place for them to winter than it was for humans.

Most passed along the eastern side of the lake, where a broad swath of rolling land rose to the hills. It was much steeper where we camped, among the rocks. That meant further to carry the prizes of the hunt back to our base. I did not mind at all; I felt more secure there.

We approached a herd now. Or a group that grazed separately from the main herd. "Wolves," whispered Spear Maker. Sure enough, gray shadows appeared and disappeared in the tall grass on the further side of the herd.

"They're heading them our direction," I whispered back. Whether the wolves knew we were there or not, their worrying of the reindeer was moving them toward us. Perhaps they knew we lurked but did not consider us important. They might know nothing of mankind.

The reindeer, as one, spooked and began loping in our direction. Not quickly. "They're going to get away from the pack," I said. Whether Spear Maker heard, I don't know. Duck Hunter wouldn't understand my words. "Be ready as they pass," I ordered. That they surely heard.

With luck, we could make two spear casts each, Spear Maker and I. Duck Hunter might even find the opportunity to get close to our prey. It would be good for him to successfully hunt with his new tribe. I crouched, ready, in the tall grass, one spear balanced in my thrower, the other jabbed into the ground beside me. I could see Spear Maker similarly prepared.

It looked like the deer were going to come right over us. We'd best rise so they would veer. Getting trampled was not the goal! I could see the wolves attempting to cut an individual out of what was turning into a stampede. Up I stood and made my first cast, calling out to my companions as I did so. I had the second spear ready before looking for what had come of my throw. A bleating reindeer came straight toward me, panicked on seeing my form, and made a sudden ninety degree turn. My spear went into its side.

It buckled. Where had my first cast gone? Spear Maker was standing over a downed reindeer and I could see Duck Hunter thrusting his spear into another. Ah, over there lay another. Either Spear Maker or I had hit it. It still thrashed about. Duck Hunter ran over to finish it off.

I pulled the spear from my kill and followed him. Yes, that was my spear in the animal. Spear Maker must have missed his other throw or, at least, not made a clean kill. All the deer were past us now and none seemed injured.

And the wolves had failed to take one down. We might well have been to blame for that. They slowly slunk back in our direction, following the scent of newly spilled blood. I saw Spear Maker pick something up. His other spear. He must not have connected with it.

"Four kills," I said. "Too much for us to carry back now."

"If we leave one, the wolves will take it," said Spear Maker.

"So we will give them one," I decided. "They helped us with our hunt." And we hadn't much choice, really. I turned to Duck Hunter. "You have done well." He might not understand the words. That did not matter.

We field-dressed our three reindeer and carried them back to the camp. The wolves were already well on their way to consuming the fourth. "Good luck, brother hunters," I called to them.

Spear Maker must have thought I was mad. Duck Hunter was merely baffled.

* * *

Our four transporters of meat returned by afternoon. All well at the cave, they said. In honesty, I hadn't thought much of those who had remained. I should probably feel guilty about that.

"Too late for another serious hunt today," I told them. "And I'm asking you to vote on whether to attempt an aurochs tomorrow. I'm not sure it's worth the danger." Admittedly, there was more meat on one of the bison than on several reindeer. Possibly more than on the giant elk we had taken. If we downed one, we would reach our limit for what we could carry home. It might even require more round trips.

"I'm tired of venison," spoke Lion Killer. "I could certainly go for a beef steak."

Fish Catcher was less eager. "I doubt they're any more tender. We're not going to be cutting any prime beef from one."

"True," agreed the younger man. "If we want fat and tender, we should go for a bear before they hole up."

I'd been thinking that myself. Too bad we had seen none here. "We'll rise early and hunt along the north shore," I decided. "No duck hunting tomorrow." Duck Hunter became alert. He might have thought I'd spoken his name—the name we had given him. We'd have to find out what he might call himself someday. "We can go down to the lake one more time, maybe, before heading home."

We were all tired but we sat up talking that evening. Sentries were, of course, posted. Mostly, I feared the wolves. We had a lot of meat here and that was sure to attract their attention. Perhaps it had not been wise to share with them. They might expect it again!

Spear Maker and Duck Hunter took the first watch, sitting on the rocks overlooking the moonlit lake and valley. We were but a little past our harvest moon now. It still shone brightly in the evening. The two could not converse yet though Duck Hunter had picked up a handful of words. Rabbit was persistent in trying to teach him. I was amused to hear a few of the words we time travelers had brought to the tribe among those he was learning.

Two more days here.

\* \* \*

The aurochs looked big. They looked even bigger up close. We crouched amid the tall grass, making our way toward the herd.

"Our best bet is to pop up from hiding and take a straggler as they head away from the water," I said. I couldn't think of a better approach nor could any of the others. "The bulls might or might not charge us when we do."

"We need the wolves to chase them," said Spear Maker. He could not keep a straight face as he made the statement.

"True. A stampede would be handy." I wondered if we could spook them. Get them running and they would not turn if we took one down. "Maybe we should be wolves today."

It was worth a try. We who were best with our spears concealed ourselves by the path the aurochs followed to and from the lake. They were down there drinking their fill now. Two men would wait until they finished and then attempt to spook them as they left the lakeside. Much could go wrong.

None the less, I sent Fish Catcher and Duck Hunter down to the water. I had to trust the older man to show the younger what was needed. Lion Killer, Spear Maker, and I concealed ourselves, all on the same side of the track so we might better communicate —and not spear one of our comrades. "Best to target a smaller one," I advised. "Not a big bull. And all of us aim for the one I pick."

"They're coming back," whispered Lion Killer. I didn't bother to look but I could hear the lowing and snorting of the animals. It was time our drivers got them moving faster. The idea was to leap up, waving hides overhead and yelling—and hope they weren't mistaken for Paleolithic bull fighters.

Yes, I could hear the pair hollering. The herd was milling, uncertain where to turn. This might work. Then—a trumpet. The mammoths were coming down to drink.

Marching down to drink, in single file. The herd of aurochs, as if of one mind, veered off in an inconvenient direction. "Maybe just as well," I said, rising. "At least they didn't choose to run over us. Let's go find some reindeer."

But we had to stand there a little while and watch those magnificent shaggy beasts. There were young among the mammoths, not so small, maybe, but not the size of the great adults. Cows, I assumed. I could not see slaughtering one of them.

Yet, someday, necessity might change my mind. That was the way of this primeval world.

# 35.

"LOOK," SPOKE SPEAR MAKER, pointing.

There were figures on the far side of Lake Jad. Human figures. A dozen maybe. Others crowded around us to spy out the distant newcomers.

I was debating whether we should make ourselves known to them until I saw the look on Duck Hunter's face. It was total terror. At once I kicked dirt onto our small fire to smother it. "Down, everyone! Duck Hunter is afraid of them so it might be wise if we are too." I turned back to the kid.

He pointed a thick finger at me and uttered but one word. "Eat."

I both nodded and blinked. Duck Hunter was bound to understand one gesture or the other. He got my meaning anyway. "We need to load up and get out of here as quickly as possible." I looked toward the sky. "As soon as the sun sets but before the moon is high."

"That is dangerous," allowed Lion Killer.

"Wolves will take the little ones!" objected his mate.

"The moonlight will be to our advantage, once we are over the ridge. As for the children—hmm." I regarded the young ones. They were not that numerous and the smallest children had remained at the cave with Wolf Chaser and She Bear.

"Put them all on leashes so they don't wander." That came from Fish Catcher.

"Yes, tie them to you. Let's pack up and be ready to go." And hope those men down there—whether cannibals or not—hadn't spied us. "And keep down!"

It might even be a good idea if we were all tied together. I wanted no one to become separated on a night journey. We worked in silence. Even the youngsters were hushed, knowing something was up. Neanderthal children learn caution early on.

We took up all the meat we could carry. In the end we would have to leave some. Not much. The wolves would be fed again. Patiently, the tribe awaited sunset. I peered out toward the lake now and then to spy on our newcomers. Would they see our tracks? Would they find our little boat? They might not know what it was but they would recognize it as the work of human hands. For now, they remained at the far end of the lake. They might be setting up a camp there.

"Let's go," I decided. "Keep as low as you can. Fish Catcher, you lead the way." He worked his way up the slope, attempting to remain on the more shadowed north side. This was not the way we had come in; that was too open. The only objective now was to get across the ridge and into the next valley—before moonlight revealed us.

"Snow," whispered Spear Maker, trudging at my side. He carried a huge load, much larger than I could manage.

Yes, flurries. Whether that would prove a good thing or a bad one, I could not guess. Snowfall might hide any tracks we had left. It could also be the start of a blizzard. But no, there were not many clouds. Those could have been welcome to hide the moon—

and us. There *was* a bitterly cold wind. Being on the north face of the hill didn't help any there.

Smoother going. We had climbed out of the rocky area and were in the heather along the ridge. This was where we were most vulnerable to being spied. But the light of the setting sun had faded away and the moon was yet low. "Stay down," I again reminded everyone. There was no reason to keep my voice low now. We were far away and the wind was howling louder than ever I could. Then we had crossed.

"Does anyone recognize any landmarks?" called Fish Catcher.

"Too dark," I called back. "That's about the right direction." I pointed southwest. If we couldn't find our way in the dark, we would have to watch for a convenient place to hole up the rest of the night.

But it was still early and the still nearly full moon was climbing the sky, thin scattered clouds rushing past its face. We should be able to see our way.

It wasn't all that long before we spied the cliff of the bees' nest.

\* \* \*

"With all the game to hunt it is unlikely they'd follow our tracks if they came across them," I said. "Still, vigilance would be wise."

Everyone was safely in the cave and we had not lost even one youngster. Most had thrown down their burdens and slept at once, though dawn was nearly upon us. There would be much to do this day.

"We could keep a watch near the bee cliff or at least on the ridge above it. See if anyone was coming this direction, maybe. Following us," said Lion Killer.

I agreed. "It might be wise to check. Everyday, perhaps, for a while." Once winter set in seriously, it would not be a concern. Probably not.

My feet were very cold. I hoped there wasn't frostbite. I massaged them and looked about the cave, at the sleeping tribe. It was warm enough in here. Not as warm as I would have kept my home in Tennessee, to be sure. The time had come to think about winter clothing. Something actually fitted and sewn, even if these people knew nothing of such garments. Mittens. I would need mittens.

The bee cliff. "I want to look closer at something on that cliff," I told Lion Killer. "We'll have to take ropes."

He nodded but didn't ask any questions. We were all too tired for questions. Maybe I should let Wolf Chaser warm me up.

"Don't wake me unless cannibal cavemen show up at our door," I warned anyone and everyone, and went off to my bed.

* * *

"I've sort of pieced together Duck Hunter's story," Blackbird told me. "Me and Spear Maker mostly."

It had been a long day. Work on processing the meat and hides had been of paramount importance. I had tried to sleep through it as long as I could. Now I was ready to sleep again. But not so sleepy I couldn't give my wife—the younger one—some attention. "He has enough words?"

252

"Not really, though both Spear Maker and Rabbit have been working on his vocabulary. You know, they're pretty smart kids."

"Their mom is no dummy."

"No, she isn't. Anyway, his language isn't really so far removed from the one we're using here. If one knows what to listen for."

"Hmmph."

"Yeah, I'm bragging, I guess. Anyway, it seems our Duck Hunter and another youngster left his tribe, looking for women. Or maybe they were chased out by the older men. He won't admit to that but I got the feeling that's the way it went. Along the way these others grabbed his companion and ate him. He ran and hid but saw what happened."

"Those we saw might not have been the same men," I said.

"True, but he is convinced every stranger wants to kill and devour him. The boy's been through a lot. It took all his nerve to approach the women. I don't think he ever would have made himself known if only you guys had been there."

I nodded. It was probably wise to be wary. "Even if they weren't the same tribe, it was best to avoid them."

"Agreed." Blackbird rose to place another piece of dung on the smoldering fire. Returning to our seats by the cave entrance, she said, "I believe She Bear appreciates you bringing a new male home with you."

"If you want him, you'd better make it known." I was not being serious. Not very.

"I think not. Duck Hunter seems like a nice kid. A sweet kid, even. And closer to my age by two or three years than Spear

Maker—not that that matters much! Ha, he even looks better. But he can't match him in brains."

That mattered to her? "Do you plan to choose a mate?" I asked.

"I suppose so. Someday. Ah, here comes our relief on sentry duty."

Someday. Someday would come. Tomorrow and the day after would come, and the moon would wane and wax, and the seasons come and go. This was my world now. This was what I had, a tribe, a purpose.

I had accepted it, hadn't I, while Blackbird resisted? Some part of her seemed unable to embrace this life, though she adapted to it well enough.

Enough thinking. It was time to embrace my wife—either one —and find sleep.

# 36.

I HAD TRIED TO introduce the word 'tool' and the concept behind it. Rabbit got the idea pretty quickly. I suspected the adults never would. They had no word for tool. Each tool had its own name.

They simply did not think in categories. In their minds, they grouped things along lines of causality. 'This' led to 'that' and had no kinship to any other 'this.' Perhaps that was more practical for their everyday lives.

We needed more tools. Bone led to tools and we had plenty of bone. But stone led to better tools.

For three days now, Lion Killer or Spear Maker had watched the distance for any sign of men. I had hunted a little, for some reindeer passed through our little valley. I was able to add another carcass to our larder, roaming with Duck Hunter. He had not yet adopted the atlatl, though I had presented him with his own spear thrower and shown him how it was used.

Rabbit, however, assured me he practiced with it when no one was around.

Today, I too would stand atop the cliff of the bees. And I would be lowered down its face on the ropes my people had twisted of sinew and bark. I had trusted them before; I would trust them again.

I might introduce the braiding of ropes during the cold dark winter days to come. There would be time. There is always more time, no matter how much of it we use up.

We had surveyed the distance when we crested the ridge above. That was where the pair had been keeping their lookout.

Again, no danger could be seen. There had been a light snow and it still lay on the ground. I had a suspicion it would be spring before we saw that ground again. But this was good if we feared anyone had seen our tracks. Soon enough, it would lay thick and we would no longer climb up here to watch.

"Not by the crevice," I told my companions. "No honey today." Not that we couldn't have harvested some. "Over here."

"That rock is going to make you heavier," advised Lion Killer.

"I need a hammer." I hoped I needed a hammer, that is. I held a rounded mallet-like chunk of sandstone. I could grip it with both hands and pound things pretty readily. Maybe not so much dangling from ropes, though.

I should find a source of sandstone, too, I told myself as I was lowered down the cliff. It was handy. Then my attention went to the rock in front of me. "Far enough!" I called. I was even with the dark band in the pale limestone. I reached out. It felt hard. Glassy, almost.

And solid. Could I break any off? I attempted to brace my feet against the wall and took a two-handed bash at it with my hammer. A small piece shattered off and fell to the ground below. I went swinging wildly and hoped I would not also fall to the ground below. It looked icy at the foot of the cliff, where water seeped out in warmer weather.

Hmm. I shouldn't be hitting the dark stone—which I was pretty sure was a chert of some sort—but the limestone around it. My mallet might not be the best tool for that but it was what I had. Bring something with a point next time, I told myself. Maybe a chamois horn. I took a few whacks above and below, and then a blow to the hard stuff again. A bigger chunk fell this time. Bigger but not big.

"Pull me up!" A minute later I was standing beside my rope handlers.

"You swung back and forth an awful lot," complained Lion Killer. He held out his hands. "Did a number on my palms."

Spear Maker was impatient. "Let us go down. I want to see the stone." The idea of workable stone for tools meant more to him. He was downright eager to get at it.

We found the chunks lying in the snow. They were a little larger than I had thought. And they were just what I had hoped them to be.

"Proof of concept, friends," I said, holding them up in each hand. "We have a source of flint."

\* \* \*

To be sure, it was not a particularly good source of flint but it was better than none. We could go back and attempt to knock some more loose whenever it was convenient. Now, Blackbird and Spear Maker were huddled over the stones, examining them, deciding how best to work them into useful objects. Duck Hunter stood watching for a while before losing interest.

There might be more of it hidden within the cliffs or it might be but that one small vein. We could not mine for it; that was far beyond the capabilities of this tribe or perhaps any other. There were quarries elsewhere, I knew, where flint was abundant, where it lay open and easy to gather. This was not the season to search for such sites.

And others might know of them. I was not eager to make contact with those others. Not yet.

Blackbird came over to where I sat musing. "We will need to gather more birch bark," she said.

"We need to do all the gathering we can, while we can. Fire-wood. Grass for bedding before it is all under the snow." I looked up at her. "How about a foray into the forest? Tomorrow, if the weather is good."

"Just we two?"

"Everyone has other tasks to keep them busy." I didn't add that I wanted to scout out the neighborhood bears. They should be holing up for winter by now.

Spear Maker went with us part of the way in the morning, before turning to take up his watch-post. As soon as he disappeared, I turned to Blackbird. "Now you can see inside our cavern without him knowing. Spear Maker would not approve of a woman being in there."

"I have been wanting to get a look. Oh, and you're carrying torches. You planned this."

I had, but I said, "I thought we might need to poke into a bear's den." It was not far to the cave entrance.

I could see it had been dug out some. "Well. We just may have found one of our bears," I remarked. "It might be necessary to cancel the underground tour."

Blackbird did not like that at all. "Let's at least look into the first chamber." She giggled. "Quietly, so we don't wake any sleeping bears."

If a bear—or more than one—was hibernating in there, it might be too sleepy to notice our intrusion. I still didn't like the idea. I lit my torch, and poked it and my head in. "No bears," I reported. I slid back out and tied a short length of rope around a nearby boulder. "I want to be able to get up and out of that hole quickly if need be."

She followed me in, down the short slope, to the globe-like chamber of the bats. I slipped and went down on the floor. "Ice," she commented.

I only grunted. It was a good thing I had more than one layer of leather to cushion my fall. "Not a good place to sleep." I held my torch high. "I believe the bats have moved deeper."

We did the same. Blackbird was suitably impressed by the next room. I was more interested in the fact that it felt warmer. Far from warm, but warmer. And that there were no bears in it. No bats either.

"The water isn't frozen here," my companion pointed out.

"I doubt it will stay that way all winter," I replied. "Still, I could see a bear sleeping here. Not sure if one could fit through the passage to the rest of the cave." I waved my torch in the direction of the opening. It did look small. But no— "Oh, there was a dead bear in the sinkhole in there. I guess one can get in."

She looked at the hole too. "I don't think I want to be trapped in there," the woman decided. "And I don't think I want to look at the place Jad died."

I understood that. Both thats. "Let's get on to the birch trees then. But I do think I'm going to bring some of the guys back here to see if we can take a bear." Maybe the sow and cub we had spotted once. Maybe the youngster we had encountered more than once.

"A minute," Blackbird said, and examined one of the stalagmites and then another. "No." She shook her head. "I'd hoped there might be some chalcedony formed here when you mentioned these. Let's go." Shortly, we stood again in the wan wintry light.

The woods looked different, the trees barren of leaves. The little pond had formed a thin sheet of ice and drifts of snow lay in all the shadows. We returned to the cave before dusk, laden with birch bark and branches.

# 37.

THERE WOULD BE NO more nuts gathered this year. We had stores of hazelnuts and acorns, some walnuts. The pine nuts had tended to be eaten almost as soon as they were extracted from their cones. The cones themselves were saved as fire-starters.

We also had dried meat in plenty. Enough to get a tribe through the winter? I had my doubts but we might just make it on our stores. And we would hunt, if we could. Certainly we had at least another month before we might be completely snow-bound.

Not that I intended to be. I would work on fitted clothes for myself, for my companions. I might even attempt snow shoes. There was too much else to do right now, the last preparations for the cold to come.

It was known now that all the women were pregnant. Wolf Chaser might be giving birth as early as February. Giving birth to our child. The rest of the pregnancies could extend on into midsummer.

The children would be half-Neanderthal, except for Black-bird's. The women here would assume Jad was the father. I don't think the fact of his homosexuality ever quite sank in for them. Oh, I suppose there was an off-chance that the two of them actually had sex. They did spend a lot of nights sharing a bed.

But it was far more likely Fish Catcher had fathered her child. I knew it wasn't me, anyway! That would be a secret only the three of us would share.

Soon we would learn whether those Modern-Neanderthal pregnancies were viable. That was but an answer to one question. We would still have to see how those children developed—whether they would survive to be healthy adults. Others would have to see how it played out in further generations.

I would be recognized as father of Spruce Tree's child. It could have been any of us, even Jad. Maybe when the births came we could better estimate when the conceptions took place. It did not matter at all. Or looks might tell us something but, again, it didn't matter.

Except maybe when this next generation sought mates.

* * *

"It is the young bear," reported Spear Maker. "The boar you shooed away." He had been checking the hidden cave from time to time, as he went to peer east, watching for human intruders. "I have seen him come and go, preparing for his sleep."

"Catch out go," said Duck Hunter. "Eat kill." His language skills were improving.

Yes, surprising the beast as it emerged would work. I couldn't think of a better approach. "So we go and wait for it to stick its head out?" I asked.

"It might be like the ground hog and not be seen till spring," commented Fish Catcher.

"Ground hog?" repeated Duck Hunter.

"A marmot. It's true, we might have a long wait. We won't even know if it is in the cave or not." I didn't particularly want to go in looking for the bear.

"I put sticks across the entrance," Spear Maker informed me. "They will tell when it comes and goes."

I wished I'd thought of that. The boy was going to rival me as chief one of these days. "So we go bear hunting at dawn," I decided. "We might need to go more than once before we find our opportunity. Make sure you have your spears ready."

Blackbird had been sitting nearby, listening to all this. The Neanderthal women wouldn't have thought of intruding on their men's hunting plans. They could do that later when they had them alone. Blackbird, however, felt no such restraint. I somewhat hoped her attitude would rub off on the younger girls.

I certainly think it had some on my Wolf Chaser, but she was inclined to be a freer spirit than the others before ever we travelers arrived.

"I've made up a new spear point," she said now. "Using some of those antlers we have in such abundance."

We certainly had a great many reindeer antlers. Unfortunately, we couldn't pack all the ones out we had gathered at Lake Jad. They were useful for a variety of tools and weapons. Ornaments, too. I might try carving one if I could find the time.

"It's an idea from a later date," she went on. Our Neanderthals had no idea what that meant. "Instead of a big hunk of stone, one can fix a small flake of flint at the end of an antler or bone spear point." She held forth a spear made in exactly that way.

"Saves on flint, huh?" asked Lion Killer.

"And that little flake can be replaced," Blackbird told him. "Glue in a new one when needed. The antler part should last a long time. It is a renewable resource, too." She looked us over. "So which of you is going to be the guinea pig?"

"Guinea pig?" wondered Duck Hunter.

"A very little marmot. I guess it's up to me," I said, taking the proffered spear. But I might save it as my backup on this coming hunt.

\* \* \*

I wondered where the female and her cub had gone to den. These hills might be riddled with suitable caves—suitable for bears. Maybe not for humans.

Maybe next year we would see them. Maybe the cub would be big and fat by next autumn and we would stalk it, even as we were this one. Spear Maker assured us it was inside the cave; we waited now on either side of the entrance, hoping it would not spy us as it emerged. If it emerged and hadn't begun its winter-long sleep. A cliff wall rose immediately above the hole so we could not get back any further.

It was not so high a cliff, more an outcropping of limestone. One might be able to cast a spear from its top. I decided, however, it was better to be close, to all throw together and then close in to finish the bear, if necessary. I had hopes it would not be necessary.

So we waited, pressed against the rock, on this cold overcast morning. I suspected more snow was on the way. Maybe the really heavy snow I had known would come eventually. The snow that might put an end to much of our hunting.

A few reindeer still straggled through our valley. A few late fliers dropped into the pond before heading off again to Africa or Sicily or wherever they found warm waters. Some of these we took.

"He comes," hissed Spear Maker. I readied spear and thrower. At the last moment I had decided to use Blackbird's innovation for my first cast and reserve the traditional flint-headed spear for what might follow. I wanted to be able to depend fully on my backup.

The bear would be most vulnerable when he was only partway out of the narrow opening, unable to move quickly one way or another. This we had decided, though he would make a better target were he completely emerged. If we didn't immobilize him quickly, he would emerge anyway! The heavy head appeared from the dark, the nose sniffed at the air. Would he catch our scent? Two massive paws, the thick shaggy shoulders. A moment more—

"Now!" Five spears flew. The great bear roared with pain, retreated slightly, and then bolted from his lair. He did not seem at all incapacitated by the shafts protruding from his flanks. I readied for another throw but my incautious companions were closing in with their spears, getting in my way. The bear rose onto his rear legs, head swinging back and forth. No one was willing to move in. Certainly not me.

Duck Hunter leaped quickly onto a narrow ledge above the cave entrance and launched himself, spear first, at the bear's back. The beast bucked and roared, trying to swat at the young man. With equal agility, he jumped to the ground and scurried out of reach. Blood rushed from the big animal's nose, his mouth. With a cough, he collapsed to the dirt.

"No more spears," I ordered. "We don't want to ruin the pelt." And there was no reason for more. It was most definitely a deceased bear. An exceptionally large deceased bear. He had put on size since we had come face to face among the blackberries. Did I feel a bit of a loss at his death, this companion of our summer? Surely. But the tribe must eat.

"I salute you, Brother Bear," I said. I turned to Duck Hunter. "From now one," I told him, "I name you Bear Stabber."

# 38.

BEAR STABBER HAD BEEN eyeing Blackbird. I think he felt more confident with a successful hunt and a new name. A man's name.

We feasted, celebrating the taking of the bear. I felt more confident too, more confident of our survival than ever before. There was plenty of the fat-rich meat to go around this night, and plenty to preserve. That it might harbor dangerous parasites I knew. There was nothing to be done about that; only some would be cooked and perhaps not that thoroughly. That was simply a fact of existence here.

Was our amorous young Neanderthal thinking to make his move? He was standing, occasionally taking a nonchalant glance in his intended's direction. I was pretty certain Bear Stabber would, sooner or later, work up the nerve to go sit beside her. I was pretty certain Blackbird was aware of this.

It would have to be done before the meal ended. When people sat side by side at other times it meant nothing more than that they wished to converse. He took a tentative step forward. Blackbird rose from her place.

And went to sit down beside Spear Maker. He did not object. Indeed, he beamed. A dejected Bear Stabber sat.

"I expected that," spoke Wolf Chaser, on my left.

"Me too," said Spruce Tree, at my right.

I can't say I was all that surprised myself. "I wonder what Dusk Light thinks of it," I ventured.

Spruce Tree shrugged. "Won't care."

Wolf Chaser seemed to agree. "She Bear will like it."

"Yes. She wants Bear Stabber herself."

The wife on my left giggled. "She hopes he stabs her."

Spruce Tree only looked puzzled by the remark. Metaphor was not her strength.

Blackbird came to sit with me as I took a watch by the cave entry that night. "So you made your choice," I said.

"You and I both knew I would eventually. I like the kid well enough." She looked toward where he slept, deeper in the darkened recesses of the cave. "But I might not be completely faithful. I'm going to be out of commission for a few months anyway."

"Spear Maker can grow up a little more before he becomes a father."

She nodded, somewhat solemnly. "Yes, my child needs someone to call father."

"It looks like I'll have two of them to do that. There's no telling whether Spruce Tree's is actually mine, though."

"Just look for those lynx eyes of yours. You'll have another crack at her before she's too old, I reckon. Neanderthal women may have remained fertile longer than moderns." She wasn't being nearly so serious now. That didn't last. "You know, maybe I should sleep with all the males to create more genetic variation and be certain of healthy children—now and in future generations."

"I'm inclined to let that be as it will," I told her.

"I'm not. Don't be surprised if I make a booty call on you a year or two from now."

"And present Spear Maker with a child with lynx eyes?"

She only laughed and went to find her new husband.

* * *

True to my wives' prediction, She Bear claimed Bear Stabber a couple nights later. With Fish Catcher's blessing, it seemed. "Her sister didn't really like sharing me," he confided. "And, honestly, I didn't like the situation that much either."

It goes without saying that Bear Stabber accepted the woman when she seated herself by his side. I'm saying it anyway.

Outside, the snow grew deeper. Rocks and dirt were piled up till the opening to our home was barely large enough to crawl through. This opening had apparently always been plugged with brush and grass, tedious to remove when anyone entered or left. Lion Killer and I made up a frame to hang hides across it, better blocking the intrusion of the cold.

Our bodies and a small fire kept it bearable inside. Warm, even. The acrid stench of unwashed bodies did grow, as did the pervasive ammonia reek of the latrine which was unlikely to be cleaned out until spring, but one becomes accustomed. Some. And it was dark. No lamps or torches burnt. That made work more difficult than I had expected. I added lamps to the mental list of projects. Bear fat should burn nicely.

The bear pelt was awarded to Bear Stabber. She Bear would keep warm this winter. She might have coveted it as much as the boy, I whispered to Wolf Chaser one night. She told me I was bad to think such things and that she agreed.

We still hunted. So did the wolves. I had hoped they might follow the herds south. But there were the deer that always lived here, and the horses. Game for both two and four-legged hunters. It was to be hoped the four-legged would not hunt the two-legged.

Through the dark days I tinkered with some of my ideas, often assisted by Lion Killer. We put together serviceable snow shoes and traveled as far as the bee cliff on them. "I don't think we'll need to look for visitors again this winter," he said as we gazed east across the snow-clad hills.

"But we can't forget they are there." I had been thinking about that from time to time. "It might be well to move the tribe else-where, come spring. To the west."

"The hunting trip to the Tiber you've mentioned? The 'great stream' as they call it?"

I know I didn't look too enthusiastic about that idea. I didn't feel much enthusiasm for it now. "There might be as much danger there. It seems that is where the tribe's men disappeared."

He nodded. "It's a dangerous world. A beautiful one too." Lion Killer looked into the white distance again.

"And a damn cold one. Let's get back."

* * *

"We must be near the solstice," said Lion Killer.

Spear Maker did not bother to turn his head toward him as we trudged through the snow. "Solstice? Where is that?'

"Not where," I explained. "It is a time of the year."

"When the sun begins to return from the south," added Lion Killer.

"Will Great Bear wake up?"

270

"Not yet. There are still moons of cold to come."

He accepted that. Bear Stabber did too, for he made no comment. I thought he understood us well enough. The four of us hunted southward from the cave. Fish Catcher rarely joined us on these longer expeditions. That was as well.

I felt warm enough, wrapped in layers of skins and furs. They were not truly tailored. Real sewing was beyond me. Not the sewing itself but the making of the needles and thread needed for such intricate work. Maybe with time I could produce something usable but time was better spent elsewhere now. My clothes, and those of Lion Killer, were fitted as well as possible with thongs, laced through holes pierced with a bone awl. This was technology the Neanderthals already had and they were skillful in its use. We had mittens and hoods. Our two young Neanderthals eschewed such luxuries and wore their hides more loosely. We all had enveloping deerskin robes—or perhaps they could be called capes —over our other garb, reaching as near our feet as possible.

On all those feet were snow shoes. These the Neanderthals had not at all minded adopting. Bear Stabber had also given in on the use of an atlatl and now carried one, as did the rest of us. We followed the stream as it turned more to the east. "There Lion Killer slew the lion," Spear Maker told Bear Stabber, pointing to the rocks at our left.

Bear Stabber glanced back at the man. He had seen the lion's pelt in the cave. Lion Killer had wanted to wear it but Last Star insisted they use it to cover themselves at night. I had noticed she usually had her way.

"Many many tracks," said Spear Maker, his mind having moved on even as we moved past the site where the lion and Fat Bear had met their ends. "Rabbits. Maybe we should set snares?"

"If we could be sure of getting out to check them," Lion Killer said. "Deer, too?" He perused the indentations in the snow.

"Horses," I told him.

"Good eat horse," felt Bear Stabber.

"Maybe we'll find out someday. We haven't succeed in spearing one yet." We pushed on. The stream was still liquid; its flow was too rapid to freeze completely, even where ice extended far out from the banks. "I assume the herd comes to drink sometime."

We could find a spot they frequented, maybe, and ambush them. If not today, there was the rest of the winter. It would beat sitting in the dark cave.

Suddenly, Lion Killer's arm shot out. "Got it," he breathed. A large, mostly white rabbit lay transfixed by his spear. The day wouldn't be a complete loss. We had ascended the narrowing, ever more rocky valley to where the spruce grew.

"I want some of these," I announced. I'd been thinking some more spear shafts would be welcome, though it hadn't been a specific goal for this day. The boughs would be nice too, for our bedding. They'd be a remedy for some of the unpleasant odors in the cave.

And just now, another idea had found its way into my mind. I wouldn't mention that yet—but I did tell my companions I wanted to carry a certain small spruce home in one piece.

We were on our way back to that home, laden with spruce and the gutted rabbit, when Bear Stabber uttered a low, almost growling, warning.

Around us moved gray shadows, in and out of the rocks and scrubby trees.

# 39.

WE AT ONCE THREW down our loads and cast off our outer robes so they would not impede the use of our spears. I was uncertain whether to take off the snow shoes as well. They might hamper quick movement.

More than the five wolves we had encountered on earlier occasions surrounded us. Another, larger pack? Or maybe more than one pack had come together to hunt.

"Do you think they would be satisfied with the rabbit?" asked Lion Killer.

"I doubt it." Spear Maker grunted an agreement. The wolves slowly circled, pacing. They would be cautious in the attack, not charging—not at first—but darting in to test us. Maybe even attempt to separate one of us for the kill.

*That* might satisfy them. "We need to attack," I said. We needed to let the wolves know we were the predators here. It might discourage future attempts on humans. If we survived.

There was no clear 'leader of the pack' to which we could turn our attention. Certainly, some individuals were more dominant but the old idea of an 'alpha male' had been discredited decades ago. The thing would be to target one that seemed more aggressive, that seemed more inclined to move in close.

"That one there," I said pointing. I knew wolves—unlike domesticated dogs—did not understand pointing. It would not be forewarned. "We all cast together and then rush on it immediately."

"To get our spears," stated Spear Maker.

Mostly. But also to impress on the canines that we meant business. That we were the ones attacking here. "Now!"

The wolf went down. Rushing was not very rushed, as we retained our snow shoes, but with noise and bluster we advanced and retrieved our weapons. The rest of the pack retreated some distance, watching us.

"Dead," noted Bear Stabber. "Eat?"

"I don't think so," I replied. "But I want the skin." He immediately went to work on it with a flint flake from his belt pouch. The boy was quite skillful at this, more so than any of the rest of us. I would have taken twice as long. The wolves continued to watch, most sitting on their haunches. There was some nervous whining. Uncertainty?

They might consume the carcass if we left it. "Let's get out of here," I said. Bear Stabber threw the pelt over his shoulder and we retrieved our outer robes. "Don't wrap yourselves up," I warned. "We might need to act quickly."

We did continue to drag our spruces behind us. I was not willing to abandon those. It was some minutes before we saw forms slinking behind us again. We grasped our spears but did not slow down. Neither did we try to increase our speed. That might encourage them to chase us—just like that neighborhood cur that used to chase my bicycle in another world. I saw Lion Killer adjusting the hafted ax he had made. That would be a far better weapon for close work than anything else we had with us. I should make one for myself when we got back to the cave. If we got back to the cave. Had something like this happened to those missing men of our tribe?

"We might need to toss them the rabbit," I said.

"Toss them Lion Killer," said Spear Maker, grinning. I think Bear Stabber took him seriously for he looked shocked.

"If we must," I answered. "But we are almost to a good place to climb up into the rocks. The wolves can not get to us there." We might freeze while we kept them off but we could keep them off.

I saw a couple of the closest wolves suddenly halt and sniff at the air. There arose yips and the pack gathered and began milling about. All at once, they turned toward the stream and took off. A minute or two later we heard the neighing of horses.

"Find chase horses," observed Bear Stabber.

"So they did," said I.

* * *

"It is a custom of our tribe," I announced. "Of the tribe to which we once belonged. We do this when the sun turns around to return to us."

I stepped back to admire the five foot tall spruce I had propped up in the middle of the cave, set into a mound of rocks. Its scent certainly was more pleasing than that of the unwashed Neanderthal bodies around me. Or mine, for that matter.

"The green of the tree is a promise that all the world will turn green again," Lion Killer added to this.

And Fish Catcher had more. "Now we must decorate it." He

hung a strand of what I recognized as vertebrae from a large trout, on a bit of string, on the tree.

"Decorate everything," I said, dipping my fingers into a clam shell and painting a streak of white down my chest. In the warmth of the cave, most wore no more than our loincloths much of the time. Sometimes, not even that much. I handed the container on to Spruce Tree.

We had the dark ocher, as ever, and black made from ashes. No more than those yet. Maybe we could find some other pigments next year. A red ocher felt like a possibility.

Others got in the spirit of our celebration, streaking themselves with color, hanging necklaces and rawhide thongs and whatever else they might have on hand in the branches. Grass-stuffed balls flew back and forth. We had a bit more fire than usual. Not exactly a Yule log, but a few branches, some dung.

This was our Yule. Our first Yule in this world, perhaps the first Yule this world had seen. It was right to have a bit of light in the cave tonight. So what if there would be months of darkness yet?

This was the time to feast, knowing the warmth, the sun, would return, this cold time would not last. It was a time to sing and to tell stories. A new year was on us, though these people did not grasp that, perhaps. That did not matter. We could spend those months of darkness preparing for it. Yes, it would get colder yet, almost certainly. But then it would get warmer.

Spring would come and, with spring, birth. Birth outside, birth in our tribe. The world being made new. Would we move on then? Would we seek a better place in this young world?

These things I could not answer; not right now. This was my better place tonight. Here with my tribe, my wives, my friends.

* * *

Months of darkness. The cave lay in darkness now, most wrapped in their sleeping furs. I sat by the cave entrance, not ready for sleep. Some slight draft of cool air filtered in around the grass and the hides; a reindeer hide wrapped about my shoulders kept me warm enough. Nut Grass sat with me, attempting not to doze off. The party had been too much for the lad.

Maybe this coming year Nut Grass's initiation would be in order. The year after, more likely. That depended on whether the boy showed signs of puberty, not any count of his age by years.

And more boys and girls after him, the tribe growing and pros- pering. Yes, as a race the Neanderthals were 'doomed' but it would be more than twenty thousand years before they were absorbed into and replaced by the modern human stream already flowing out of Africa. That was so in the world we had left—who could say how things might play out in this time stream? The few genes I and my companions had contributed might mean nothing or they might be passed along, changing these people. I wouldn't be here to find out.

Wolf Chaser came out of the darkness. "Your other wife needs you to keep her warm," she whispered. "I will watch here. You go too, Nut Grass. Wake up that lazy Spear Maker." I embraced her, holding her body, the body that held a life we had created within it. A kiss and I went to a bed made fragrant with boughs of spruce.

# Afterword

So we reach the end of the tale of our time travelers. The end of one chapter? Perhaps; we'll see if there is more to be told one of these days.

The poem at the front of this book was part of the inspiration for my story—for the title, at least. This one of my older pieces and has been published in my collection 'Dreamwinds.' Available, of course, from Arachis Press. But I've been interested in our ancient ancestors for a very long time.

As far as I know, my narrative is a reasonably accurate portrayal of the time and people. Research only goes so far, and we must recognize that there would have been no one 'Neanderthal culture' for a people who ranged widely for hundreds of thousands of years. Much has to be guess work and some was certainly guessed incorrectly. That is inevitable.

Be as any of that may be, I do hope you have enjoyed 'When Man Was Young' and I thank you for reading it.

*Stephen Brooke*

www.ingramcontent.com/pod-product-compliance
Lightning Source LLC
Chambersburg PA
CBHW030033030726
47500CB00001B/85